MARDI GRAS
MURDER

Edited By Sarah E. Glenn

Mystery and Horror, LLC
Tarpon Springs, Florida

Mardi Gras Murder
Edited by Sarah E. Glenn
Copyright © 2014 by Mystery and Horror, LLC
Published by Mystery and Horror, LLC

ISBN-13: 978-0989007689
(Mystery and Horror, LLC)

ISBN-10: 0989007685

Printed in USA by Mystery and Horror, LLC
(www.mysteryandhorrorllc.com)

Dedication

Mardi Gras Murder is dedicated to two of Mystery and Horror, LLC's strongest supporters: Deanna Familton and Lena James. Their love of New Orleans and Mardi Gras inspired this title, though we sincerely hope their trip to this year's celebration is murder-free.

TABLE OF CONTENTS

———————

EVEN
BY
DANIEL MOORE

It was just after midnight. Witches cackled on St. Peter, clutching onto knockoff hand bags and pint glasses filled with a neon pink brew that stunk like cherries and sugar. I winced, kept my face low, gave them a wide berth. Turning onto Bourbon, more of the same waited for me, stumbling in and out of Savage Kat, yapping over their drinks and laughing at deafening levels. Across from them, a world away, was home, the Old Rose.

I pushed though the side door of the two-story brick-and-mortar block with my right shoulder, the good shoulder. My left still clicked under the weight of my tool bag. I wondered if it was dislocated, if only a bit.

Heavy bass and electric keys jammed on the other side of the wall. Their purpose wasn't to fill the room, but to lift the velvety voice that accompanied them, to help it climb above all their instruments. And they did. Each syllable that formed came from a songbird I could imagine at home in an age of wax records and highballs and stogie smoke. For a moment I paused in the dark corridor, the secret entrance. I heard the song kick up, the voice crescendo, and ultimately fall. The claps broke my concentration. It was their last set of the night, I was sure. I turned from the sound and walked down the stairs.

Alphonse, the black kid, the new kid, no more than twenty-two, was stacking and bonding the bills the counter spat out. He entered counts into a spreadsheet on a computer tablet, splitting his attention with math and the game playing on the wall-sized screen at the front of the room.

1

I nodded in his direction, and he threw up a hand in acknowledgement. I asked for the boss and pointed to his office. I walked on, headed to the back of the basement.

Past a row of splintered doors and hanging bulbs, around walls of aged brick and French plaques, was the old room that once belonged to the slave of a rich Spanish cartographer who mapped The Quarter a couple hundred years back, or so Barnaby said. I didn't believe him. Don't think anyone did. It's not like he was the first man in Louisiana to lie about his estate to seem more important that he already was.

I knocked on the heavy oak door and pushed through before I got an answer. Even after seeing his office so many times before, it still seemed too big. I doubt a cartographer could've afforded enough space for Barnaby to fit his spy-villain motif of dark oak furniture, stocked bar, and the never-touched entertainment setup that curved around the room.

The boss waved me over while he listened to the blinking earpiece fixed on his ear, melting into the pink flesh of his fat, bald head. He was crestfallen, cradling his face in his hand, trading drags from a kretek with a sip of cognac. I kept my distance from the desk, left him finish listening to whoever was giving him grief on the other end.

After what felt like an unhealthy pause, he grunted something in the affirmative and tapped the plastic device. The lights around his ear died. "People make this job difficult," he said. He downed his glass and pointed to the chair. Ginning, he said, "Beau, tell me, how'd it go?"

"Simple. No troubles." I lied. The evidence was in a taught shoulder that bit me in protest at every step. I took to the high brown leather chair at the foot of his desk and dropped down into a state that felt familiar to comfort. "I got the samples, cleaned up the scene, set the stage. They should figure it out right away."

Barnaby smiled with the black smoke stick held between his perfectly square teeth. He held his hands out like a greedy asking for his gift. I lifted the bag as gracefully as I could, tried not to show the fatigue that had sapped me of all will except the desire to sit and breathe.

2

Unzipping the black leather, Barnaby said, "I want a recap."

"What for?"

"The job came as a favor—"

"I don't get paid in favors, Barnaby."

"You won't," he said looking me squarely in the eye. "But the job came in as a favor and the client wants the details of how it went down. It's a personal thing for them."

I huffed, intent on protest, but I quickly folded. Said, "I identified him by the pictures, the tattoo on his neck, the Jenny that sat across his throat."

Barnaby nodded his big head, took out tools by handful, the lock picks, the gloves, the rope, and arranged them on the desk, around the Japanese-cased computer cube, the box of smokes imported from Singapore, and the old-world English lamps.

"I staked out the house for two weeks, made notes of when he was alone, when the girlfriend came over, when the wife got home. Today had a lot of lag in his schedule, so I went in and got it over with."

"Did you do it like they wanted?" said Barnaby, taking out the red plastic case from the bottom of the bag.

I nodded. "Left the toy on the bed, the computer on the website you said." I leaned onto my good arm, fished out the micro card he had given me weeks back. I tossed it to him. "Ran the program you said, added the fake internet history."

"And him?"

"Black belt from the ceiling fan. Didn't think it would hold him, but I waited about ten minutes, watched him. He swung a bit, but he wasn't going anywhere."

Barnaby flicked the case open. The glee of a job well done washed away. He was serious now, let down almost, like learning the truth behind an illusion, learning that there was no magic there, just pieces of theater to make things seem as they ought to instead of how they were.

Barnaby snapped it shut and placed it in a steel bucket he kept on the floor, this time filled with ice. "Good. I'm glad we got this one behind us. I know I've been keeping you busy lately, and

3

I promised you more work right away, but the next one seems like it'll be a little ways off. I'll let you know if that changes."

I was relieved to hear that. I needed a bit to mend. Said, "That's all right." I planned for a full day of sleep, aided by a handful of painkillers, the kind I bought from the skinny tweaker who worked the midnight shift in the pharmacy on Royal. I decided I'd stop there before heading home, buy enough pills to put me out for a handful of days.

"Go upstairs," said Barnaby, "tell what's-her-name to pour whatever you want, and get some food, please; you look like hell. I'll have the kid bring you your check once he's done with the books."

"I think I'll just wait it out down here."

"Are you sure?" he said with an oily smile. "You know she's singing tonight."

I didn't know how he knew, but it was the carrot needed to get me out of my seat.

Everything on me felt like a bruise, the aged kind that felt less intense with pressure and movement. So I climbed through the employee entrance up to the kitchen. Felipe was busy firebombing two of the cooks with angry Spanish. I didn't speak it, but by the look on their faces, I could tell that he couldn't either. The cooks nodded their heads and rolled their eyes, cursing him in secret.

I walked past the scene, to the double doors that pointed to the bar, the main floor, the source of bass plucking away at my ear. Then I felt energized, wanted a drink, and food didn't sound like a bad idea either.

I sat at the bar, ordered Jack and ginger from Madeline, the girl with the short pixie cut. She knew me, the way I took my drinks lately: more booze than soda, light on the ice, a skinny wedge of lime. I chased a sedative feel.

In the middle of my second sip, feeling the cold on my lips, the speakers kicked up, knocking away the low hum of bar chatter. Lenny, Theo, and Carlos were gone. The old jazz trio, their music, the place's vibe switched over to this new kick Barnaby had been featuring for weeks. He claimed the club was losing money, said something about appearances, maintaining a public image, boss stuff. So a new act was hired; new headliners with a younger feel than the old-world music that dragged me in here for the first time years ago.

The band was experimental, kitschy, something that tried to be edgy and cool in equal measure. I had seen them before and didn't care for their sound. But what did capture my attention was the woman who stood center-stage. She always worked on me like magnets. Her voice wasn't particularly special; she was no Billie, not even Amy, but she caught my attention whenever her lips parted and sounds poured out. I didn't pay attention to the music or the words, I heard nothing, I just watched, drank, and ordered more.

Three songs sung and Alphonse emerged from the kitchen, dressed in a leather racing jacket, a red and green helmet in his hand. He dropped it in front of me and sat one stool over. Flagging down the black pixie cut, he said, "Wild Turkey Sour." Madeline spun around and went for the bottles before she reached us. He leaned over to me and said, "Barnaby wants you back here in two weeks, Friday night."

I felt every muscle in my body tense up in protest. Would I have enough sleep between then and now? I wondered. "What for?" I said.

"He said that he got a call, that he's got work to hand out."

I dug in the helmet, pulled out the envelope. I didn't count it; the weight felt right, and I doubted Barnaby, knowing who I was, would try to short me. I slid the helmet back to the kid who took time with his glass.

I turned around in my seat. The club had been emptied out. The new band was wrapping up, packing up more computer equipment than instruments, which made for quick work. As I made my way for the door, I saw her spot me, like on other nights, pierce me with green eyes that seemed mechanical, inhumanly bright under thousand-watt bulbs of shifting color centering on brown skin. Normally I'd nod in her direction and leave, but this night was different. Maybe it was the intoxication from exhaustion, the feel of a good payday, or the six glasses I had finished, but I didn't feel the need to exit like I normally did. I simply stood there, sporting a dumb grin, watching her pack coils of cable and MIDI controllers and a silvery laptop. She looked up, smiled equally dumb.

She said, "Hi." Her accent was thick, southern, the kind that mad I'm sound like Ah'm, and turned sugar to shugah. It made me smile.

"Hey," I said, surprised at the absence of slurring.

She laughed, at first, and then pulled back. "I've seen you here a lot, haven't I?"

"Yup, you might have. I work here."

"And what is it that you do here…"

"Beau," I jumped in, thinking my own name sounded false for a moment. "I'm the bouncer," I lied.

She chuckled in a way that sounded like music. "A jazz club needs a bouncer?"

"Sometimes."

"You see a lot of trouble here, Beau?"

"Sometimes."

We were silent for a moment, comfortable, beneath the blue and yellow spotlights. I felt the club around us quiet down as cleaning was underway. I felt the need to talk. Said, "Where are you going now?"

"At three in the morning?" she said matter-of-factly. "Home. Why?"

"'Cause I wanted to buy you a drink, maybe get you to sing a song for me."

I watched her zip up her bag, hand it off to the kid with the shoulder-length blue hair, the bassist, and step off the stage. "For the Old Rose's bouncer," she said, "I could have a drink. But I'm done singing for the night."

I grabbed a bottle and a pair of glasses from Madeline. We sat at a table in a dark corner. We drank and talked, waited for the sun to rise. Her name was Eveline.

I woke under a mane of golden brown curls. The smell of smoke and perfume filled my nose. She draped over me, legs wrapped around, fingers digging into my sides though she still slept. The time from when we met to that point had melted away, as if it had passed in the blink of an eye, a dozen days folded on

6

one another, dropping us both into oblivion. I didn't mind, didn't care about the world beyond. Far as I was concerned, all that mattered was breathing on my chest.

Then the phone buzzed.

I turned about, annoyed, looking at the glow flashing on the ceiling. I reached for the phone on the bedside table and read the screen. "Shit," I whispered, careful not to wake her.

I tried to slide out, slow and quiet, but she sensed me move, clenched her fingers tighter before letting me go. Eveline recoiled into a sleepy curl in the center of my bed. She looked up with half-opened eyes, radioactive green piercing the night. "What time is it?" she said.

"Almost nine," I said, slipping out from under sheets.

"What day is it?" she smiled, climbing out of covers, bare breasted.

"Friday."

"And we spent the whole day in bed?"

"Not the whole day."

"Where you going?" she said, running her fingers through her hair.

"I've got to get to work for a couple of hours."

She sucked her teeth. "Call them, tell them you're sick."

"I would, I want to, but I've got to be there for a meeting. I'll be back soon."

"A staff meeting in a bar...." Her voice drifted off.

I said nothing, grabbed my clothes, my keys, and dug under the bed for my shoes.

"Do you want me to stay?" she said.

"I do, but only if you to."

"I do." Wrapping herself around me, she squeezed, pulled me back down to a pile of pillows. "You can be ten minutes late, right?"

I grabbed the .45 and holster from the glove compartment, stuffed it in the waist of my jeans, and followed Alphonse down the hidden door on Bourbon Street. Quiet as always, the kid delivered Barnaby's discontent in as few words as possible. Said, "He almost sent me to get you."

"Got caught in traffic. Did we start already?" The kid nodded. "You have a feel for what this is about?"

"No," said Alphonse as he pushed through the basement door, "but by the looks of the guy we won't be getting paid shit. I'm pretty sure on that."

Sitting at the counting table, watching the Pelicans take a beating from the Pistons, was a uniform, over-the-hill cop, managing his gut bulging over his gun with his hand, pinching his waist higher as he adjusted himself in Alphonse's chair. Like a bad allergy, I felt my skin redden, turn paper-thin. Reflex shot my hand to my back, wrapping around the rubber grip.

Alphonse's walked on ahead, looked at me over his shoulder, said, "See? We'd be lucky to get anything for this one."

Barnaby, at his office bar, poured whiskey, black label stuff, into a glass with a generous heart. He grinned ear to ear, an expression I didn't think his face could make. He slid the drink over to a man in a tailored suit, the kind that screamed for attention, said he wasn't a man of money but a man who thought himself important and happened to have money. A rat's stench poured off of him. My allergy flared up.

Barnaby spotted us, opened his arms in celebration, spilling booze all over the place. "There you are. Quick, come in, we've got work to discuss."

Alphonse hung back, locked the door behind me. I felt like a dog cornered. In my head I rehearsed an exit back to the car.

Barnaby pointed to the cop, said his name was Philip Morrow, Sergeant, 8th district, hero. The last detail sat in my mouth with bad taste. Morrow had been plastered on websites and cell screens for months, so they said. I wouldn't have known. His claim to fame came with the rescue of two small girls, twins who were prisoner at the top floor of a warehouse overlooking Lafayette Cemetery. "A big bust," Barnaby went on, "Philip's been cracking down on these... what did you call them?"

"Traffickers," said Morrow.

"Right. He's been taking down these traffickers down left and right. In the past year he's made two dozen arrests in the city. Makes sense the city's putting him on a float. It's all a big build for the announcement on Monday when they make him Lieutenant."

"Congrats," I said dryly. "So this is why you needed to meet, Barnaby?"

"Actually," Morrow cut in, sipping from his glass, stealing my momentum, "I asked to meet with you. I saw your work. The guy with the tattoos over in Holly Grove, the one who touched himself to death; was that you? I'm impressed because we didn't find anything out of place."

I looked to Barnaby, felt Alphonse standing behind me. The gun was burning hot. The keys weighed down in my pocket. I wondered what I'd have to do if running was the only way out. And for a moment, just one, I thought about Eveline.

"You've been doing this a long time?" said Morrow, sliding the glass back to Barnaby.

I stayed quiet. Barnaby moved in on my behalf. Said, "Mr. Celice has been working for a number of years now, and I'm sure that he can handle this problem of yours. Why don't you give him the details of your problem?"

Through half a bottle of Town Branch, I stood and listened to Barnaby and Morrow going back and forth about "old days," a time when the officer made money watching the boss' back while they moved vials and capsules of poison across the state. It was good for business, good for the cop's pockets, but his partner, Jacob Morin, thought different. In a time before me, they handled the situation as best they knew how. Unfortunately for Morin, the burns were so severe that it took the NOPD weeks to ID him; long enough for Morrow and Barnaby to hide the ties that led back to them. But the job was done and with it the message traveled through the precincts and eventually all over the city. Moral cops kept their distance. Morrow was untouchable.

Now, Morrow had become a victim of his own infamy. Operating without scrutiny, protected by the badge, had made him a success, but with that success came envy. Frank Lopes, a fellow officer, same rank, by-the-books cop, had been overlooked for his turn on climbing the ladder to Lieutenant. It didn't take long for him to hear that Morrow would be getting it, and it took even less time for him to step up. Morrow and his mud-covered history were in peril, but only one thing stood in his way: a white hat with a badge.

After he explained all he could, he took a deep breath and pressed the glass to his head. I could see it in his face, beneath the fake smile, the reminiscing, he was crumbling. I enjoyed it for a moment. Said, "So what do you want me to do?"

"Fire," he said, looking at me serious, ignoring the ounces of booze in his system. "It has to look like he died because of a fire."

My mind snapped keywords into a history of other jobs, quickly stopped on a dozen scenarios that could work. "And when do you need this done?"

"Tonight or tomorrow, any time before my ride on the float tomorrow night. He threatened to go to the press with this if I didn't reject the parade offer from the Mayor. He gave me till tomorrow afternoon."

"What am I looking at?"

Morrow turned to Barnaby. I'd confused him.

"Payment," said Barnaby.

"How's forty? But that's if you get it done tonight."

I huffed, took a step closer. "Give me the address."

I let Alphonse drive as I ripped the towing strap out of its plastic casing. I took the cardboard backing and ripped off bits of plastic, leaving nothing but bright blue paper advertising Harry's Auto Parts. I stuffed them both in my coat pocket and rooted around the back seat for the blow torch.

Alphonse slowed down, tapped me on the shoulder. "Magenta house at the end of the street," he said.

I could spot it; so could everyone else. I didn't like that. It opened the door for variables.

We waited for hours, for the street to empty, for the lights in the house to turn out. Eventually they all did, and I could track Lopes, moving alone in the dark, his shadow bleeding through plastic blinds. I waited for the black car creeping behind us to turn the corner before I climbed out.

10

Turning to Alphonse, I said, "Keep it running. I shouldn't be more than a few minutes." He listened, turned the key over, shut off the lights, switched to drive, and held his foot on the brake.

Climbing in through the kitchen window, I took my time scoping out the ground floor, marking flammable surfaces, low hanging fabric, cooking oils, all to act as accelerants. Seeing everything I'd need helped me plan out the burning while I turned up the stairs to the top floor.

TV glow poured between the cracks of a partially opened door onto faded carpet. I could hear cheap karate chops over exaggerated acting. The low laugh of a sleepy man told me he was in bed, entertained by ancient kung fu recorded on old, scratchy film.

I inspected every door in the hall, looking for other bodies. There weren't any, just a pair of bathrooms, an organized guest room, and a closet with untouched weights and a dust-covered treadmill. All the signs of a sad single life.

Standing around the corner from the luminescent door, I knocked hard, hard enough that he wouldn't mistake it for anything else. Stirring and groaning drowned out the clang of swords coming from within the room.

Lopes walked out, groggy, wiping his eyes clean, ignoring my shadow falling onto his face. I lunged out when he passed, wrapped the strap around his throat, and pulled. Lopes scratched at the thick nylon weave, managed to hook his thumbs in, started to pull away. I crossed my arms, turned my back to him, and leaned his body on mine. The weight and pulling turned the choking sound into intermittent gurgles. Swinging in midair, he left his throat and tried to bash me with the back of his fists, to hit the walls with fury, anything to catch the attention of anyone outside the home. But nothing he tried worked; his arms didn't reach too far back, the lack of air made his fists land with soft taps. He then stopped, went limp, and I waited until I felt his lungs deflate against my back.

I was exhausted for the first time in years. I couldn't explain why. I looked down at his soft blue face, the saliva that wet his mouth. I wondered if I would need to wipe it or if the fire would handle that for me. Then, out of nowhere, her voice entered my head, singing a poorly written song. I felt sick.

Placing Lopes back in bed, I quickly wrapped him up as though he were readying for sleep. I snapped a picture of him with the cell. Then, using the chrome handheld torch I boosted from the kitchen, I lit the cardboard and tossed it on the bed. I went on to light the sheets in his bed and curtains in his room before getting the rest of the top floor and doing the same to the living room. The fire spread fast, leaving only the kitchen untouched. I returned to my window, knocked over a bottle of oil, and lit the short white curtains before slipping out and tumbling on the grass.

I looked at my work, hypnotized by the destruction of flames, the consumption by fire, how fast it had grown, how angrily it licked the glass with tongues of black smoke.

The bushes behind me rustled. I turned. The gun was already in my hand. It was only a cat, small and brown, her hair standing on end, running away from danger. Smart, I thought. I took a final picture of the inferno, then followed her lead.

It was a quarter to midnight, and Barnaby and Morrow had sobered. In Morrow's hand was a black plastic bag where the glass once was. I told him we were done, showed him the pictures as proof. He handed it to me, and I to Alphonse, told him to count it, twice, take his ten percent and bring me the rest when he finished.

Morrow and I climbed up the kitchen entrance, following the sounds of a sad piano and scratching records. I curled my face in disapproval, though pleased because I recognized Eveline's voice.

"So you've been doing this long?" said Morrow, now that we were out of earshot from Barnaby's office. "How do you get started doing this kind of thing? You don't seem like some punk who pops people for a couple hundred dollars. You must have a story."

"I don't tell it."

"That wasn't a prompt. I probably wouldn't want to hear it anyway. But I would want to hire you again." He dug in his

12

breast pocket and fished out a tan card, his name and rank printed in gold engravings. "Call me in the morning if you're interested. I can provide a steady flow of work for you."

I took the card, though I did not want to. Then I heard the voice, the average, unimpressive voice, *her* voice climb high on the back of a rising note. I turned from Morrow and went out the double doors, shoving the card in my pocket.

Eveline, bathed in violet light, made love to the microphone while people swayed around her. She opened her eyes, saw me, and smiled. It was contagious. Morrow walked by, causing me to move further into the crowd. Her voice cracked and she shut her eyes again. I made her nervous, I thought.

One a.m. approached fast. Eveline's band finished, and something more jazz friendly took their place.

She found me at the bar. I had Madeline prepare a glass with her in mind. She downed it quick. She grabbed my hand and said, "Take me home, your place."

I did.

Eveline was quiet the whole way there, keeping her eyes fixed on the window, the blurring concrete outside, the drunks daring themselves on Tulane Avenue.

In bed, she felt different, touched coldly, tasted wrong— who was she? Eveline clamped on, got tight, made an effort to move again, but her head was a million miles away. There was no desire to continue, no want to reach any high. I sat in my own bed, stiff, holding her till she fell asleep. Then I rolled over and did the same.

Given the past couple weeks, waking up early was surprisingly easy to do. I didn't like the feel of that. I didn't like the sight of her back, clothed, turned to me. I wondered what had gone wrong.

Down in the kitchen, I made coffee, caught up on the news, and ran the dishwasher for the first time in months. I then got changed and ran for three miles before the sun rose. I was budding with energy and nowhere to place it.

When light finally touched ground, enough to wake the rest of the street, I stepped out the front door with a cup of black and three sugars, took the phone along, closed the door quiet, not wanting to wake her. I dialed Morrow.

"I knew you'd call," he said through a mouthful of food. The sound of munching on the other end conjured a joke about cops and donuts and I somehow believed it was still appropriate for cops who contracted hitmen. "Did you sleep well? I mean, after that whole nasty business I know I wouldn't be able to."

I sipped coffee, letting the pause ride, teaching him about boundaries, what you could and couldn't ask a contractor. Said, "You claimed to have work for me. Is that still the case?"

Papers crumpled in the background, the wound of wax sheets, the kind used to wrap drive-thru food. "It is. Give me your cell, and I'll text the details sent to you."

I shook my head even though he couldn't see me. "Best I can do is an email; send the details in an attachment as a .zip file."

I imagined him grinning and nodding on the other end, loving his time playing in the N'awlins underworld, taking a step above slinging dope and muscling out other cops. "I can send that to you," he said. "And if you can get this done before Monday, you can expect double the commission."

Morrow was really loving it. I took another sip, paused for effect. "I'll see what I can do." I hung up the phone and finished my coffee, watching the cars speed. Everyone was having a productive morning.

Walking back into the house, I heard a noise, and then I quickly realized it wasn't a noise but rather a continuous stream of sound, an acoustic rustling projecting from the speakers in the living room. I thought of Eveline, thinking she woke in better spirits, killing time with some internet video.

I skipped past the kitchen and down the hall. The rustling grew louder, clearer, a crisp crackling. Then I saw it, flames, my screen consumed entirely by fire, a savage burning that tore through magenta walls and lit grass on fire. Then I saw me, hopping out of a kitchen window, turning around, looking at the lens before snapping a picture of the scene.

The picture froze.

I couldn't turn from the sight, not even when I heard the gun cock. The familiar sound of the .45 I carried with me at all times vibrated through my bones, lighting up memory receptors in my brain. I looked at the hall, my only exit. I wondered if I had the energy to run out the door after my morning run.

"This is what you do?" I heard her say. "You burn people in their sleep?"

I turned around, slow, hands up, hoping she was close enough to grab the gun. Eveline stood on the stairs, a dozen feet away, about six vertical, holding the gun like she knew how. I then realized she absolutely knew how. She pointed to the screen with the tip of her nose. "Did Morrow pay you to do that?"

Hearing his name fall out of her mouth rattled me, but I held it together. Said, "I don't know what you're talking about."

"You're really going to play denial? Act like I don't know what you are, what you do? How long have you been working for Morrow?"

"Eveline," I said with honey in my voice, "just put down the gun. You're talking nonsense, I don't know any Morrow."

"You're a fucking piece of work, you know that? I've been watching Morrow for years, that crappy little bar for months. I know he goes there, that he's friends with Barnaby. I've seen you before a few weeks ago. Hell, I have more tapes than just the fire. I've have you killing people all over the city. Name any of the people you killed since June and I have it on a secured hard drive dedicated to the vile shit you do."

My chest caved in and ribs pierced my organs. I gave up, dropped my hands to my sides, and leaned on the couch.

"Talk," she said, tightening her shoulders, taking that police-academy stance.

With a gun to my head, I told her all I knew, what little Morrow and Barnaby had told me, that he was a bent cop, but a hero to the city; that he had a parade appearance and someone wasn't a fan. But when I got to the smaller details, mentioned the fire, the one before me that charred Jacob Morin to a flaky black biscuit, I heard the sobs. I looked to a tear-soaked face. A side of me wanted to rush over, console in some way that felt human, but my legs wouldn't comply. I wasn't focused on the bullet aimed for me; I wanted to see her that way.

"Did you do that too?" she said, gritting her teeth, trying to hold together. "Did you burn Jacob? Tell me you didn't kill him in his sleep. Tell me you didn't lock his daughter in the closet when you set their house on fire. Tell me."

"I only met the man yesterday," I said shakily.

"I don't believe you," she said, choking back tears, "you're a bastard and a fucking liar, but I don't care what you are. You're going to do something for me and if you don't, that video and all the others are going on the Internet and every news site I can find. It'll only be a matter of time before they find all of the other people you killed, and then they'll gas you like they should've done years ago."

I inhaled deep and blew out slow, trying to find some reservoir of calm. It wasn't there. Hiding the nerves in my voice, I said, "What is it that you want me to do?"

"Kill Philip Morrow."

"You don't want me to do that. You don't know what you're saying."

"I do," she said, stepping off the staircase, staring around me, pointing to the PC tower hooked up to the screen in the center of the room. "What he did to Jacob, Morrow deserves to die for." She leaned on the eject button on the side and scooped up the disc that slid out. The gun was still steady as she backed up to my front door. "You have until tonight."

"He's supposed to be on a parade float tonight. It wouldn't be smart to get him before. People saw me talking to him and leave with you. It would put a lot of suspicion on the both of us if he goes missing before then. Not to mention, the Mayor's expecting him for a big announcement on Monday. It'll have to wait until then."

"No. That's when I want you to do it, when he's on the parade float. Tonight. I want everyone to see him die. If he's alive, if I have to see his face on a single screen after the parade, alive, then I will post this everywhere and you'll run out of earth before they find you. You won't get away. Not this time. After all the people you killed, you'll go away for killing a cop."

Eveline's voice burned my brain. "Why did you follow me? Did you plan this out?"

"You don't deserve sympathy, Beau. Don't pretend that this isn't just. For you, for what you are, this is more than fair."

I swallowed sharp, a pane of glass cutting the inside of my neck. Said, "How do you expect me to kill him during a parade? A hero cop that saved two little girls is going to have a lot of eyes on him."

Eveline shrugged. "This is what you do for a living, right? This is what you do when you're not bouncing, right? You figure it out."

"If you're forcing me to do this, I'm going to want that video when it's done. I want that whole hard drive."

"Do your job first, and then we'll talk."

"How do I find you?"

"I'll call you."

I watched Eveline eject the clip, pull the slide, and toss my gun across the room. I followed pieces flying overhead, only for a moment, but it was long enough. She was gone.

Fighting the urge to run after her and hide her somewhere until I could disappear, I walked up to the door and turned all four locks. "Fucking great," I said to myself.

Another cup of coffee and a smoke introduced a stimulant overload that evened out my heartbeat; matched my nerves and shaking hands by trembling them at the same frequency. I tried to remember the last time I was nervous. The memory, wherever it was, had been deleted long ago.

I walked down to the basement, my personal workshop. I thought about Morrow, floats, and screaming crowds. It was going to be a trick for sure. A public killing always was.

I looked around the room, explored my options.

Under the tool bench were a few packs of Semtex, 1-A, the quality stuff imported from Israel. A brick of the red plastic was enough to blow a hole in any float and rip him in half. Provided I could find the right float in the hours before it took off, it could be an option. Casualties were optional, probably preferable; bombs make people think terrorism, not hits. Confusion would help me get away.

I looked ahead, to the small assortment of guns I kept on the wall. In the center was my .45 ACP, a match to my constant companion, a reliable black number that took little maintenance. On the left was the Franchi SPAS I got for security when I found one of the kids from the neighborhood trying to sneak in a back window. The sound of a racking shotgun was enough to send them packing and never come back. And seated at the right was my Vintorez, an ancient Cold War Russian piece. In truth, it was little more than a hand gun with a rifle's stock. But the gas propulsion made each shot silent and travel at a distance comparable to a Dragunov. From a balcony overlooking the parade route, I could see myself take him down with a shot; clean, quick, quiet enough for me to get away. It made more sense than a bomb.

February skies made blue skies gray, showing signs of rain. I wondered if that would change things. The crowd thinned, shoved themselves indoors, into the surrounding bars. I took the advantage, ran with it.

I squeezed between buildings when no one was looking, worked the lock on the side door of Miguel's Bistro. The place was so packed they didn't notice the man in the ski cap and olive jacket climb their steps to the for-rent suite above them.

The place was deserted. Moped, shined, and waxed, waiting for its new owners to approve. So long as I didn't overstay my welcome they wouldn't mind.

Lying on my stomach, using the rolled up jacket as support, I watched the crowd mingle among the music and sounds of night. What wasn't colored in sickeningly bright flashes of gold and pink light was washed in blue and white paint covering, most of it covering skin. It seemed not even the temperature could fight the one-time-a-year nudists.

Leaning on the Vintorez, propping my chest off of the balcony floor, I looked into the scope and traveled down to the felt eyes of Sir Saint. The gaudy purple float turned down Chartres Street. The mascot swung his big chin left and right, tossing plush footballs, paying particular attention to the painted breasts in the crowd. The people responded with even more energy, causing the crowd to frenzy, to beg for more beads.

I had been listening to Eveline's vibration-inducing anxiety from the earpiece linked to my cell. She had called, claiming she needed to hear it happen, needed to know it was me, the fear of an unknown, an anticipated something, that made her cells vibrate like a paint mixer. It was throwing my calm off balance. I blocked her out, focused on the videos, the end to an otherwise methodically guided career.

"Are you sure you can do this?" she said.

"Are you sure that this is what you want done?"

"I need this done."

"Just tell me where to find you."

"After. I don't trust you while he's still alive." Eveline fell silent. I imagined her pressing the mute button on her screen.

I leaned into the scope again, looking down at a fast-food king tossing out plastic coins with Zeus' angry, Greek face. He wielded a garish white scepter and got more followers than the big-headed mascot. The people flashed him more skin, too.

Then, at the end of the block, came an eyesore of simplicity, a float devoid of the fun, festive, borderline perverse displays of the dozens of floats that came before. A simple platform of blue and white streamers, playing a Queen song I couldn't pin down. Definitely not a single, some throwaway B-side that never got much attention, but Mercury's voice was unmistakable. In the center of the float, wearing a gray and blue suit, was Morrow, shielding his eyes, at night, with bejeweled plastic.

I centered in, adjusted the digital zoom to his upper torso. I could hear Eveline's breath increase. And then, as if I had blocked it out before, I noticed the sounds of the street, the cheering, Mercury's voice come in stereo. The bitch was on the street. I pulled back, observed the street as a whole, and there, mere feet from my position, behind an aging, curved tree, hiding in a cluster of women, half-dressed, half-painted as pirates, I saw her. The thick brown mane and her large green eyes shot me back to my bed, with her legs wrapped around mine. Then all I could

19

hear was her breath in my ear, and then all I could feel was her lie.

The parade pulled up and a frantic, but muttering voice urged me to get on with it. I pulled from her and back to the parade. Morrow waved, ignoring that no one paid him much mind. I pulled in tight, centered over the bridge of his nose.

"Where are you?" she said. "Why haven't you done it?"

"I've got the bastard," I said. And through a beaded tear I focused. I pulled the trigger.

Daniel Moore is an author from New York City. He writes post-modern fiction in the noir and cyberpunk subgenres set in the sprawling metropolises of the modern day. Moore's work can be found in online and print publications, most recently in Chiller 31. *Daniel Moore currently works as a freelance contributor to several journalism outlets.*

QUEEN OF THE KING CAKES
BY
HARRIETTE SACKLER

Emma Tower stood near the front door of the French Quarter café and proudly surveyed the place that meant the world to her. Mardi Gras was just a week away, and the city was electric with anticipation. All the tables were filled with patrons, sipping fragrant coffee beverages and nibbling on a fantasy of pastries that had been freshly baked only hours before. Beignets, croissants, napoleons, éclairs--every manner of delicate confection that had elevated Emma's reputation as one of the premier pastry chefs in New Orleans.

But the piece de resistance, the one delicacy that resulted in media interviews and orders months in advance, was Emma's King Cakes. The delicious cake, lightly flavored with cinnamon, and sporting the beautiful purples, greens and gold of Mardi Gras, had earned Emma the title of "Queen of the King Cakes". The delicate porcelain babies, especially designed and produced for Emma, hidden deep in the heart of the confection, had become collectables and often found their way into boutiques and high line shops to be purchased at inflated prices.

Emma grew up in a beautiful old house on St. Charles Avenue. Her father was a banker who was well known as a community leader. Her mother spent her days organizing: charitable events, church functions, dinner parties for her husband's business associates, and certainly, her well-functioning home. Her parents didn't spend a great deal of time with their only child and mostly entrusted her to Carrie, their longtime housekeeper.

21

Emma and Carrie were inseparable. The child would shadow her caretaker around the house. She'd play in the kitchen while Carrie prepared the evening meal and would often help her by peeling vegetables, mashing potatoes, and shelling sweet peas. And, best of all, Emma loved to help Carrie bake the mouthwatering delicacies that graced the family's table every day.

Emma's passion for baking continued to adulthood. She'd learned well from Carrie, creating magnificent pastries and cakes. She had no interest in much of anything else. While friends married and started families, Emma wished them well, but had no interest in traveling down the same path. Her parents were sorely disappointed, but no matter how hard they tried, they couldn't convince Emma to set her sights on more conventional pursuits.

On her twenty-third birthday, Emma announced that she wanted to open a bakery and café where folks could purchase her baked goods. Her parents were appalled at the prospect of their daughter becoming a common shopkeeper. After all, that just didn't happen in their world. But nothing they said or did deterred Emma from her goal. To avoid the risk of alienating their child, they finally agreed to finance Emma's venture.

Emma's entrepreneurship was successful beyond her wildest hopes. So, in this year of 1950, at the age of thirty-three, Emma Tower had made her mark in her beloved city of New Orleans and far beyond.

One evening, as Emma sat at her desk in the pretty little office off the café's kitchen, her husband, Justin, joined her. Her parents were thrilled when Emma showed an interest in the youngest son of a fine New Orleans family. But, as it turned out, as handsome and charming as he was, his deficits far outweighed any positive attributes the man possessed. Five years after their marriage, Emma couldn't for the life of her, understand how she had been naïve enough to think that they could build a life together. Justin had a fierce aversion to any form of work and chose to spend his time in New Orleans' gambling houses. Emma had become his financier, and she'd had enough.

"Darlin', I could use a cash infusion for my evening's recreation." Justin stood behind her and kneaded her shoulders, causing Emma to shudder.

"I can't let you drain my business dry. Marrying you was a terrible lapse of judgment on my part." She, in an unusual moment of weakness, had succumbed to his charm and good looks. "You contribute nothing, nothing at all. Why don't you get a job? Or better still; give me a divorce, so I can be at peace."

"Now, sweet girl, why should I have to work when my little lady is so good at it? And, you know we can't divorce. We're good Catholics, and we'll be together until death do us part. Now, I need that money."

"I don't have it!"

Justin grabbed her hair and pulled her head back so far that she thought her neck would snap. She'd endured his physical abuse almost from the beginning.

"You give me that money," he snarled.

Emma slowly rose from her chair and, through eyes watering with pain, walked to the safe built into the far wall of her office. Her exquisite body blocked Justin's view as she keyed in the code and opened the heavy steel door. She withdrew a small packet of bills and turned to him.

"That's all I have. Take it and get out of here!"

"Thank you, my love. You certainly know how to keep your man happy. Oh, no need to wait up for me tonight," he remarked over his shoulder as he walked out the door.

Till death do us part. The marriage vow kept playing in Emma's head. It was true, of course, especially for those whose religious convictions condemned divorce. But, death could certainly come prematurely. The question was how. Could Emma, who had never hurt anyone in her life, be able to end Justin's life? Either she would free herself from a hellish marriage or live with a man who would make the rest of her life a living hell. The choice was clear.

Emma spent the next several weeks thinking, planning, and doing her very best to overcome the doubts that besieged her.

23

The thought of doing violence to another being made her ill. She never would have entertained the possibility of doing something so heinous. But, if she ever hoped to have a life anywhere close to normal, enjoying the success she had worked so hard to achieve, this seemed to be the only option open to her.

One day, it all came together. Emma knew what she had to do. Justin would disappear, and his "loving wife" would report him missing, confident that he would never be found. She spent several hours creating the most beautiful King Cake she'd ever made. She'd added additional ingredients to enhance the flavor of the mixture: rum, orange peel, lemon zest, all to hide the bitterness of the rat poison she hoped would send Justin to meet his Maker. If there was one of Emma's baked goods that he could never resist, it was his wife's King Cakes. He'd been known to literally consume a whole cake in one evening and that was what Emma was counting on today.

When Justin came home that evening after doing whatever it was he did with his time, Emma put his dinner on the dining room table.

"I'm going to spend a few hours working on invoices and then go to bed. I've got to get to the bakery at the crack of dawn to start prepping for some special orders. There's a King Cake on the kitchen counter I made with a new recipe. Let me know what you think."

"Ahhh. You know I'll have that polished off by the time I call it a night. I must say, your King Cakes are works of art."

"Thank you. The cake's for you and I hope eating it will be a heavenly experience."

Emma went up to her bedroom with a heart pounding uncontrollably. She put on warm clothes and heavy boots that she rarely wore in the Louisiana heat. Then she sat on her bed and waited.

Several hours later, Emma heard a loud noise from downstairs, then a piercing scream. "Hold on, girl, it's almost over," she whispered.

When silence returned, Emma cautiously crept down the stairs. Justin was sprawled on the living room floor, items from

24

an overturned end table scattered around him. His eyes were open and an expression of surprise and pain was frozen on his face. Blood dripped from his nose and both ears. Emma's throat closed, and she could feel her legs buckling. By sheer willpower, she steeled herself for what she had to accomplish next.

Her van was parked in the alley behind the house, ready to transport Justin to his final resting place. She opened the rear door of the van and removed a cart that she normally used to deliver pastry orders. With strength born of necessity, Emma was barely able to drag Justin's body to the kitchen door of the house and lift him, inch by inch onto the cart. She struggled to wheel it to the rear of the van where she hitched herself up until she was able to reach down and pull the body up into the van's empty storage area. Her muscles screamed with pain. When Justin's lifeless body was finally settled in the van, Emma jumped down and lifted the cart in. Then she climbed into the driver's seat and headed away.

Emma drove slowly and cautiously out of the city. One thing she knew for certain was that the gators that inhabited the Louisiana swamplands had voracious appetites and could make wildlife or humans disappear in quick order. How many newspaper stories had she read about the poor souls who lost their way amid the foliage and waterways, and were never seen again?

When she reached her destination, Emma stopped the van as close to the water as she could. She left the headlights on to deter anything coming too close. With great effort, she pulled Justin's body out of the back and let it drop to the ground. He certainly was beyond pain. She rolled him to the edge of the swamp until he was immersed in the black water. With no backward glance, she got back into the van and drove away.

She focused on one thought: this was the beginning of a new life for her. She was finally free.

"Good morning, Miz Emma. Time to get ready for your special day."

The wizened old woman awoke and opened her near-blind eyes. She squinted at the young woman standing by the side of her bed.

"Good morning to you, dear. And why is this a special day for me?"

"Miz Emma, it's your birthday! How does it feel to be 96?"

The old lady contemplated the question for a minute, and then chuckled. "Oh my! My birthday? I stopped keeping track of that long ago. But, to tell you the truth, I'm not feeling a bit different than I did yesterday when I was 95. I do believe that just waking to a new day is special, though I'm not so sure the good Lord is doing me any favors by keeping me on this earth."

"Now, Miz Emma, I don't want you talking like that. You're our elder stateswoman and very much loved around here. Now, I'm going to give you your breakfast in bed, and then we'll get you up to dress, so that you can greet all your admirers."

Emma Tower sat in a soft, cushioned chair in front of the window that overlooked a small garden. Although she couldn't see the individual flowers she'd took such pleasure in over the years, she could just about see the colors of the bountiful blooms. At her age, Emma knew you had to take pleasure in whatever little things could put a smile on your face.

The nurse had helped her bathe and dress in a clean nightgown and robe, both in the lavender color she was partial to. Her hair was neatly combed and rolled into the bun she'd worn for as long as she could remember. A hand-crocheted lap blanket was draped over her knees, since no matter how warm it might be, she still felt a chill in her fragile bones.

Emma closed her eyes and retreated to the place where she spent most of her time these days. A time when she was younger, and she thought the future was wide open with possibilities.

Unfortunately, Emma's plans did not conclude as she had hoped. How could she possibly know that a group of gator trappers would arrive early the next morning at the exact spot

26

where Justin lay? Although swamp creatures had begun to feast on his remains, investigators had no difficulty identifying Justin. An autopsy clearly determined that his death was a homicide, resulting from poisoning. Stomach contents of a large amount of King Cake sealed Emma's fate.

At trial, neither the judge nor jury were moved by her account of the abuse she'd suffered at the hands of her husband, and quickly found her guilty of first-degree murder. She was sentenced to prison for life without the possibility of parole, a punishment far worse than death as far as both Emma and Judge Hardy was concerned.

She remembered the judge looking condescendingly from his perch on the bench.

"Mrs. Tower, you have committed a reprehensible crime. To violate your sacred marriage vows by knowingly taking the life of your husband in such a heinous manner is beyond this court's tolerance. I will not sentence you to death because I truly believe that a life in prison is a penance you will suffer far longer."

And on that very day, Emma was transported to the living hell of Angola, one of the most feared and dreaded institutions in Louisiana. Life was so harsh at the "Farm" that its inmates, both women and men, aged quickly and died of the heat, exhaustion and hopelessness. Just at the point when Emma was at the lowest point of despair, she and the other female inmates were transferred to the Louisiana Correctional Institute for Women, a new facility which afforded them somewhat more comfort and opportunity. Emma continued to live one day at a time, and as the years passed, she transformed from the youthful, talented woman she was to an old woman.

All through the day there was a steady stream of visitors who came to wish Emma Tower well. They all had received special permission to come to the infirmary to spend time with their matriarch.

"Why, Mary, I love this beautiful blanket. Your crocheting is so fine, and I do thank you for thinking of me."

"Sylvia, did you make this lovely vase in the ceramics shop?"

"Why Annie, what lovely fruit! One peach will last me for days!"

Emma loved these women. She had mentored so many over the years and had laughed and cried with them over news from home and farewells as they left and returned to their families. Many returned to visit with Emma, but for others, prison was something to put behind them.

Emma had finished her dinner and Nurse Charlotte was helping her prepare for bed. The sun was setting outside her window and, as she did every evening, Emma wondered if she would see it rise again the next morning. At her advanced age, she couldn't take anything for granted.

The door to her room opened and a statuesque woman entered. She was middle-aged and well put together. She exuded an air of authority, but her expression was one of kindness.

"Emma, forgive me for not coming to visit sooner. It's been a very busy day and, truth be told, I wanted to be sure I had good news to brighten your birthday."

"Why, Warden Rogers, how nice of you to come to see me."

"Emma, I have something to share with you, something I wish I'd been able to tell you years ago. But I guess it's better late than never."

Emma's questioning look indicated she had no idea what the warden was talking about. Wasn't her friendly visit enough?

Warden Rogers kneeled in front of Emma and took her hand. Had Emma had better vision, she would have seen that the warden had tears in her eyes.

"Emma, it is my pleasure to tell you that the Governor has commuted your sentence. Your years in prison are over. You're free to return to the outside world."

The old women thought that for sure she had finally succumbed to dementia.

"Warden, I ....I don't understand..."

"Emma, dear, you'll be leaving this institution and transferring to a lovely nursing home in New Orleans. It has the most wonderful reputation for the care it gives its residents and its well-maintained building and grounds. You will live the rest of your life as a free woman."

"But, but, Warden, this is my home. I have no people left on the outside, I've outlived them all. I have no money and couldn't possibly afford what it must cost to be in a first-class nursing home."

"Emma," the warden smiled, "you have more than you know. Many years ago a fund was established by your many supporters and it's been growing every day. You have enough funds to live in high style in New Orleans."

Emma was speechless. After so many years, a lifetime, she would be free.

A thought entered her head, and she looked at the warden in wonderment.

"I can go to Mardi Gras again?"

"You bet you can, dear Emma." The warden wiped at her eyes with a tissue, but her voice reflected the deep emotion she was feeling.

"Oh," the warden's voice cracked as she lifted a box from the table next to her.

"I've brought you a birthday present with warm wishes for a happy future."

Emma opened the box and gasped." Dear Lord, I haven't had one of these in over sixty years."

Her near-blind eyes shone as she gazed down at a beautiful King Cake.

Harriette Sackler serves as Grants Chair of the Malice Domestic Board of Directors. She is a past Agatha Award nominee for Best Short Story for "Mother Love," which was published in Chesapeake Crimes II. *In 2013 "Fishing for Justice," appeared in the Sisters in Crime-Guppies anthology,* Fishnets. *"Devil's Night," a tale of life in a ruined city, can be found in* All Hallows' Evil, *a Mystery and Horror, LLC anthology.*

Harriette is a member of Mystery Writers of America, Sisters in Crime, Sisters in Crime-Chesapeake Chapter, and the Guppies.

She lives in the D.C. suburbs with her husband and their three pups and spends a great deal of time tending to her duties as Vice President of her labor of love: House with a Heart Senior Pet Sanctuary. She is the very proud mom and grandmother. Visit Harriette at: www.harriettesackler.com

INTERNATIONAL VOGUE
AND THE
PAJAMA FIASCO WEEKEND
BY
ROSALIND BARDEN

"If you have a problem with me, then file a complaint with *International Vogue*. I know they will be happy to ignore you."

This was my biting response to a creature that clearly did not belong in my cafe--or the one I hang out in, anyway--looking at my pajama bottoms, looking at the rest of me, and saying, "Really?"

It is important for me to explain that I normally do not go out and about in pajama bottoms, but I had experienced the worst weekend in my life and was depressed. I needed the comfort of my latte in my cafe. That *thing*, who was wearing peculiar two-toned shoes and, of all things, a tweed romper?--should have at least pretended to have a drop of human compassion at this critical juncture in my life. I would like to see how he responds to my comeback. Tweed romper, indeed!

The horrible weekend actually began prior to the weekend, at 2 p.m. on Friday, to be exact. I am often accused of being vague and all over the place, but, you see, I am a precise person. At 2 p.m., my so called friend called me to fire me from the job he got me as an audience member for the new reality-sitcom-variety/shot-live show he's a production assistant for. "They said you're not enthusiastic in a 'detached way.' They only want, 'hip, cool, non-over-reactionary cutting edge urban youth

31

metro types that viewers can hope to be some day.'" I think he was reading from something.

Oh, my, God! What? I admit I got upset. Maybe I started screaming in the phone. Can you blame me? So, my so-called friend back-tracked and said he'd talk with "them" again.

I should have known this was a ruse, but I held on to this razor thin edge of hope until he called again Saturday morning at 7:30am. *7:30am--on a Saturday?* I want to make the time clear-- again, being precise. He was at work, maybe even never left. Can I tell you I am so glad I never got accepted for all those hundreds of production assistant jobs I've applied for?

"They want people who are 'very clearly young, 20- something's only.'" Knife to heart. Knife to heart. I *am* 20- something. As the no-mercy, no-come-back, sheer cliff drop off of thirty looms ever closer, doesn't he know that I am afraid? Doesn't he know the free fall off this horrible cliff keeps me up at night?

I flung my phone to the floor. It smashed--and now, how am I supposed to buy a new phone if I have no job? I hate that guy.

I pride myself in my masculinity. In my head shots, especially if I allow a touch of stubble to shadow my craggy chin and cheekbones, I come clearly across as strong, powerful, leading-man. But I also know that being a man is loving myself. Loving myself equals being honest: I spent hours in bed sobbing. Yes, this strong, craggy faced, powerful head shot, was sobbing. Before you judge, this will be a useful experience for me to draw upon when I start getting the serious, meaty, Oscar contender roles I should be getting as soon as I find a manager who isn't a complete crook, like that idiot in the apartment next door.

My next-door neighbor isn't the only hateful person in this building, which must be cursed. It was another awful neighbor I ran into later in the afternoon after I noticed a cockroach scuttling across my tear-stained face. That made me realize I better crawl out of bed, scoop up the trash in my place, and venture out to the trash chute in the hall.

He saw me poised at the chute with me holding my trash in my arms and using the bottom of my tee-shirt to help support the mess because I ran out of trash bags awhile back. Oh, and lest I forget, I was in pajama bottoms and was wearing rubber flip flops from Rite-Aid (yes, the one in Hollywood on Sunset--don't lie, you know exactly the one I'm talking about--don't ask me what *I* was doing there and I won't ask you what *you* were doing there).

This guy I really hate. He wears these goggle-eyed, white-frame glasses and big, spotted bow ties--all the time, am/pm, holidays included--that I guess he thinks creates a persona or something. He always has some pretty boy with him. Or maybe it's the same pretty boy, just different hairs. And he always has two leaping, yapping poodles on rhinestone leashes.

Bow-tie idiot had these poodles with him now. I was wondering why, since he lives on the floor below, and why he was walking them inside the hallway instead of outside, when suddenly I made the connection to the misty, almost-raining day outside to the poodles to the mysterious rash of dog droppings despoiling my floor's hallway to this man. Oh, how tacky can you get?

Despite what school guidance counselors told me in an attempt to destroy my life (I could write a book about the injury so-called guidance counselors have done to what should be my strong inner core), I do have a sharp mind, particularly when it comes to crime. A real knack. Why does the world not see me as I really am? I don't get it.

Anyway, I was about to fling my discovery of his criminal activity at his tittering face and demand confession, when he quipped that he was having a "little party at my place tonight, you know, to cut loose a bit for Mardi Gras. Why don't you come?" Then he and his pretty boy looked at each other and start giggling.

Oh, the things I wanted to say and was about to when my sharp mind started making connections again--like I told you, sharp, precise, lightning speed mental reflexes. This guy has some sort of job at some sort of studio doing no work whatsoever as far as I can tell and getting paid a bucket load of money. I need and deserve a job like that. If I become his friend, he can get me a job like that too.

Did I tell you I studied Shakespeare? It's all about life is art and art is life. I have made a study of the hallway lighting. I'm an expert in it, actually. So I knew exactly how to angle my face so the light caught my chin and cheekbone crags with just the right punch of imposing masculinity. Then I looked at him directly and let my big brown eyes melt into pools of vulnerability (power + soft = WHAM), and said--keep in mind, when I'm doing my deep voice, it reverberates with intense, sexy, masculinity--"I'd be delighted to."

I was so immersed in character, I forgot about the trash me and my tee-shirt were supporting, and it all dropped to the floor. The two of them burst out laughing, or as much as they could burst since they are always giggling and twittering anyway. I decided I would play it as a comedic scene, which a touch of poignancy, so smiled shyly in a Chaplinesque way. And then I walked away.

My height is one of my strengths--my *many* strengths, contrary to what school counselors and my crook of an ex-manager would have you believe--and I was not about to let my height be diminished by bending and picking up trash in front of the bow-tie idiot my sharp analytical mind had discovered could be my ticket to My Life in Hollywood. Also, I couldn't possibly see how he and pretty boy could have an issue with my trash since they are having their little poodle dogs poo everywhere in the building, except probably on their floor. But they did: "He just left all his trash!" and more laughing.

This got me upset all over again. But, you see how quality my acting skills are that I ignored them, stayed in character, until I rounded the corner. Then I collapsed to the floor in front of my unit.

I was trembling. Had I blown it? It occurred to my strong intellect that when people invite you to a party last-minute-like, it means you're not really important and it could be half-joking and you're not really meant to come. Oh, God, what was I supposed to do? On top of this, I had no idea if I'd left my door unlocked for the trash run, or if I'd locked it and dropped my keys with the trash pile and how could I go back and dig through the trash with *them* still lurking around? I could hear them speaking baby-talk to the poodles, encouraging them to make a big poo, "for your daddies."

At that moment, I heard the door to the apartment next to mine open. Instinctively I cringed, expecting my crook former manager to emerge and laugh at me, like he usually does. Instead, out came his starved and trembling girlfriend, who is also his client. I always forget her name. It has an "l" or two in it so I think of her as Ding-a-Ling. You can tell how successful his management skills are by the eviction notices that appear regularly on their door. Okay, I get those too, but we're talking about them now, not me, so let's stay focused.

"I thought I heard you," she whispered. She didn't lock her door behind her. I know that, because he doesn't let her back in if she does. He calls that, "training her to remember things like keys." Why did I ever let this negative energy person be my manager?

She tested my door--it opened!--because she knows I always forget whether I've locked myself out. With this anxiety item crossed off my list, my body relaxed.

She sat down next to me, her starved eyes as always, popping out of her face. "You were crying for hours. I heard you."

My heart was touched. I still talk to Ding-a-Ling because she cares like no one else has ever cared about me. Well, maybe my mother, but can we not go there right now?

My tales of woe poured out of me, culminating with the latest incident, the party, the idiot in the bow tie.

"Oh, you've been invited too?"

Excuse me, why should she be so surprised? I wanted to feel annoyed, but then she's the only sympathetic person in my life.

"Danny [my ex-horrible-manager-neighbor] says maybe he can make connections there to get me a job. He says I'm just not motivated enough and I'm getting too fat, and that's why he can't find me work. We were almost evicted last month."

No kidding. "I keep telling you to ditch him. He charged me all that money, and for what? He got me exactly zero auditions, zero work. I have a knack for criminal investigation and he is one. He ripped me off."

"He means well. He's so fragile. I need to stay with him and help him. He can't survive without me. I know he'll be really successful. I just have to be more supportive of him."

She was getting that defensive tone. Well, I'd heard all that before and then some. Bow-tie idiot's pretty boy once cattily told me she was a porn reject Danny scraped up from the Valley somewhere, so maybe all things considering, Danny was an improvement. Whatever.

Time for me to take off. But just before I vanished into my abode, she said, "I need to run to Rite-Aid to find some kind of hostess gift for the party. Danny says they'll be expecting it and if I don't get the right one, it will blow our chances with them."

I slammed my door. Kind of in her face, but that can't be helped. Now I was in a bind. I had neither hostess gift nor any funds to acquire one. I was frantic. I dug around my kitchenette area (it's full of clothes--I look good in good clothes, so I buy-- can you blame me?). I shook the roaches off a jar of jam I bought with someone at the Hollywood Farmer's Market during idyllic more days. So many idle Sundays spent spreading this jam over hot fresh bread when life was happy and full of promise, which is why the jar was only one-quarter full. Those days are past, and maybe I should be grateful the relationship crashed and burned when it did, because at least I had some jam left to work with.

I found a 6-snak-pak of apple sauce that wasn't too expired. I stirred it into the jar with the remains of a partly drunk bottle of beer, cleaned off the jar, and we're good to go.

The rest of the time I spent preparing me. Me preparation is always time well spent. I used the last of my quality hair product, making my shoulder length raven locks shimmer and shine. How I'd pamper my hair and drop the cash back in the days when I was getting residuals from that airline commercial. When the airline changed management, I was told my "look" didn't fit with their new "branding." Excuse me? My pilot character gave off such a reassuring aura of confidence and safe flying, I'm sure my chin alone must have sold millions of tickets. I hate that airline.

But I still have the chin, the craggy cheekbones. I left the stubble because I'm out of funds to get new razors, but it works out anyway. Gives me that hard, animal look. On with excruciatingly expensive tight-tight black pants and tight-tight off-white ribbed turtleneck. The residuals ended before I could blow equal cash on decent footwear, so I went barefoot, which I often do. It's part of a semi-Jesus, semi-animal persona I've been trying out.

I have never skimped on mirrors in my pad, so I'm always able to do a final spin around to check the effect. Shazam! I must say, and I'm not bragging, I am *cut* and *tight*. Even though my gym membership was repo'd, I still get a hard core workout bench pressing canned goods at home. And people say I don't know how to make do?

The party was packed, spilling out into the hall. Bow-tie idiot barely looked at the jam jar when I explained it was special "beer jam, artisan made, from the Hollywood Farmer's Market." I felt so insulted, given all the work I'd done.

I scanned the crowd. There was Ding-a-Ling being dragged about by Danny. Looked like he was chastising her about something and she was on the verge of tears. Nothing unusual going on there. The rest of the crowd looked like pretty boys and club kids. No serious Hollywood types. I was working up to indignant fury at bow-tie idiot for wasting my time getting all fabulous for these useless types, and him pointedly ignoring me on top of it all, when in walked a boring looking suit and tie. Well, now. Agent? Exec? Clearly not a club kid, so must have possibilities. All eyes were on the suit. Danny was creating a wave of chaos pushing Ding-a-Ling through the crowd toward him.

I lost the suit in the crush. A pretty boy tossed glitter on my head. Another one threw beads over my neck, and yet another handed me a mask: "To look mysterious, my love," he said. The mask had rhinestones and feathers. It didn't look too cheap. I guess bow-tie idiot was laying out the cash for his do. Another kid with blush brushes behind his ears and makeup all over his hands offered to, "Paint you up like a hot, sexy vampire?" No, thanks. I don't know where those hands have been. Also, vampire does not mesh with my persona.

I wore the mask, the beads, the glitter, because I felt they enhanced the semi-Jesus, semi-animal persona I have been toying with. When you're starting out in entertainment, whether an actor or not, it is vital to brand yourself with a persona. This is something that airline should have thought more deeply about before pulling my ad. With a persona, people remember you. You get a rep. A, "Oh, yeah, I saw him at that Mardi Gras party. Everyone knows him." Then, you're okay to be hired. Get me? Critical.

I worked through the crowd thoroughly and let me tell you, there were no other possibilities than that suit. I caught a brief glimpse of Ding-a-Ling talking with the suit, alone, before the crush pulled me away. Then I saw Danny on the other side of the apartment by the kitchen talking with his animated smile face to someone who wasn't the suit. Too much hair and female, besides. She was absolutely covered in glitter, like that ridiculous club kid painted it on. Tacky. I recognized that animated Danny smile face. He only wears it when he's hustling. Probably trying to sign her and get her money. I should warn her, but I have my own problems.

Then Danny was alone with the suit and his animated smile face was definitely tucked away. He looked furious, even. Then bow-tie idiot was draping beads over the suit, then a group of boys wearing badly home-made papier-mâché heads and nothing else surrounded him. Wise words of my wisdom: If you don't have anything to show, don't. I could get away with such display, but, of course, have way too much class.

I was determined to get my minute with the suit. Then, I'd blow this Mardi Gras. The pawing pretty boys were getting on my nerves. No one messes with my threads or my hair.

After one particularly rambunctious set of hands tried to do away with my pants, I decided I needed to retreat to a quiet corner to regroup. I was shocked at how much bigger bow-tie idiot's apartment is compared to mine. Like triple the size. I remember someone telling me that the top floor, where I live, used to be "servants quarters," so the units are smaller than everywhere else. I was so insulted since I like to think of my pad as a penthouse. But now, I wondered.

I found myself by a little bathroom that was serving as the ladies room for the party. Since the ladies were scarce at this Mardi Gras, it was a quiet zone. Across from the bathroom door was a large-ish closet that wasn't being used as a closet. It was glammed out in blinking Christmas tree lights and purple fabric draped along the walls. I suppose that was Mardi Gras decor or something. It was just big enough for a purple beanbag, so must be the make-out spot.

And lo and behold, on the make-out beanbag, in the dim blinking lights, was none other than the suit. Maybe he was trying to escape the pretty boys, maybe he was looking for a pretty boy to make out with him. Whatever! Resourceful as always, I seized my opportunity.

"Hi, I'm Josh McConnley." Oh, by the way, that last name is one I've been trying out lately. Goes with my persona. Very strong, masculine, yet, sympathetic. I used my extra deep, animal voice.

He didn't say anything, but that's typical. The power players don't talk to you until they deem you worth their valuable time. Okay, I'd go with it.

I told him about my time studying Shakespeare in Pasadena, about my time in my high school drama club where no one appreciated how much more talented I was than them. Of course I highlighted the airline commercial and pointed out how stupid the airline was. When the airline dumped me, the agent I had back then dumped me too. She said she was keeping my bad luck from "spreading." That led me to discussion of my father.

He still didn't respond, and I noticed he must have passed gas or something because he really was developing an odor. But, hey, I was going with it.

And, you know, no one has ever listened to me for this length of time. I was touched, and realized this man is one of the few in Hollywood with a caring heart, who understands talent.

I was in the middle of telling him this and explaining that I have been holding out signing with an agent until I met someone exactly like him, when Ding-a-Ling emerged from the bathroom. She looked like she had been crying, which is how she usually looks. She stared pop-eyed in my direction, which is also typical, but instead of shyly saying "hi," she gasped and zipped away.

I turned to the suit to remark on how rude some people are, but then was taken aback by how he looked with the glare of the light from the now open bathroom door shining on him.

"Someone did a really crappy makeup job on you. Are you supposed to be a vampire? Those club kids are so ridiculous. Here, let me fix it."

I was about to do some artful smudging and blending with my thumb, which I am expert at (I studied at the Hollywood Makeup Academy until, well, we won't go there just yet), and was in the process of wondering why he had the tail end of some Mardi Gras beads hanging out of his mouth, when there was a scream. It was another woman, about to go into the bathroom, but I guess she had to pause to see who was making out in the closet. And this causes her to scream? What planet did she fall off of?

But then there were other people and they were screaming something, words like, "Oh, my God! He's *dead*!" and so on.

Now I was screaming. My hand had just about touched his face, but I leapt back like lightning in time to save my hand. Did I tell you I have athletic reflexes?

It was my cue to be gone, so I fled (again, the athletic reflexes) out of the Mardi Gras madness and back to my pad. I could still hear the party music throbbing below, but at least I was safe from that dead person.

I had to pause a moment to be hurt and saddened at humanity when I realized the suit hadn't been listening to any of my heart outpourings because he was probably dead the whole time.

Once I recovered, my sharp criminal investigation intellect kicked in. Something told me this was no natural death. The way his face looked, so badly-applied-make-up-like and puffy. Not natural at all. But I don't think it was club kid makeup. It was too unnaturally natural for their skill level, if you get what I'm saying. My mind connected the beads hanging out of his mouth to the beads bow-tie idiot was piling on the suit. Did bow-tie idiot and his pretty boy lure Hollywood power players to their Mardi Gras parties to do them in? Jealousy, perhaps? Kicks?

As I was thinking thus deeply, I was interrupted by a timid pounding at my door. That sound could only be Ding-a-Ling. I thought about ignoring her, but then decided I needed someone to bounce my theories off of.

She fell into my arms, which alarmed me, but I was able to push her off before her mascara did damage to my shockingly expensive tight-tight off-white ribbed turtleneck.

She was sobbing and babbling about the suit, which I didn't appreciate since I was supposed to be the one talking. But, then she blurted something about the suit being a manager, "like Danny." My sharp mind picked up this clue.

"Oh, you mean like a crook that takes your money?"

"Yes, I mean, no. He charges a fee, but he has expenses, like Danny."

"So, he was trying to represent you, take you away from Danny?"

"Danny was so upset at that man. Oh, please don't tell Danny I told you! You know how mad he gets!"

Bam!

The whole scenario came to me.

I charged out of my place, into her place, which I knew wouldn't be locked because, like I said, he doesn't let her back in if she forgets her key. There Danny was, jumping in surprise, with guilt written all over him and his eyes darting around in a nervous way.

"You are the murderer! You could not stand to have, ah," and I almost said Ding-a-Ling but fortunately my strong improv abilities kicked in, "your woman leave you for another manager! In a fit of jealous rage, you killed him!"

He gave me a twisted look and said, "What? You are so dead." Which I took to be an admission of guilt.

He pushed me with his hands. But, here I was channeling Action Hero, so, chest out, I pushed him back.

He pushed me again, I pushed him, when I realized Ding-a-Ling was talking to someone on her cell phone (which made me jealous that she had an unbroken cell phone). What was she saying? Confessing?

Then the sirens and the police were up in the apartment in a flash, so I guess they don't have anything better to do. I immediately introduced myself to them with my new last name, and explained that she was covering for Danny, the real killer. Meantime, he's off to the side laughing and saying he's going to charge me with assault and battery, and she's sobbing up a storm about how Danny can't live without her and she couldn't have the dead suit guy upsetting Danny by trying to take her away.

It was the Mardi Gras beads. On the beanbag, in the purple make-out room, she shoved the beads down his throat with some kind of extraordinary tongue skill that made me see her in a whole new light, and he choked to death. She did a demonstration for the police, extending her tongue just so, wrapped in a set of beads she pulled off a policeman's hat (those club kids, throwing beads everywhere). I think pretty boy's gossip about her past work experience is correct.

Other than ordering me to take off my mask, writing all of one short sentence to record my vitally important role in discovering the body and bringing the guilty to justice, and asking me, in an insulting tone, if Josh McConnley was my "real" name, the so called police ignored me.

That was too much, so I started a verbal tongue lashing until they said something like, "Oh, so you want to be arrested too?" and laughed! Now, if that isn't police brutality, I don't know what is. I was forced to give them a name I have no emotional or life core connection with, so therefore, it is not authentic. How is that for accurate police work?

After they took her away in handcuffs, with her saying, "I love you!" to Danny, what did he do? He leaned under the sofa and said, "You can come out now!" Out pops the glitter girl he was chatting up at the Mardi Gras party. They giggled and proceeded to make out right in front of me.

Out of there! I just wanted to hide safely in my pad after all this heavy duty emotional baggage flung at me, but there was bow-tie idiot and his pretty boy being lookie loo's in the hall with half the other party people covered in glitter and wearing the masks (the police confiscated mine).

"I love that beer jam of yours. So artisan. What stall did you buy it from?" Then he and everyone laughed so I knew he was making fun of me. So what if I kind of made the jam myself? Hand-made gifts are from the heart. Since he clearly hasn't one, he is incapable of appreciating real gifts.

I didn't bother to waste my profound words on him. Fortunately, I'd left my door unlocked, so was able to open it and slam it pointedly.

I pulled off my duds, carefully--I take good care of my clothing--and put on my jammies and tee-shirt. But I couldn't sleep with the party music still going.

It was so late at night, it was starting not to be night and I noticed the sun was coming up.

I was depressed, fragile, felt disrespected, abused, brutalized, unappreciated. I realized this is how film noir detectives feel after dragging home from a night of solving particularly grisly Hollywood murders (my new persona, perhaps?). The only thing I could do was go to my cafe with the last of my meager funds, and get my latte.

That's when I encountered that *character*. The one in the tweed rompers. Okay, the tee-shirt I wore was the same one I took out the trash with so maybe had strange blobs on it. And, okay, it's sleeveless. This cafe definitely is the shaved crowd so I should have known my masculine hair on and beneath my arms, not to mention on my chest, which I am proud of by the way, might have drawn unwanted attention from rubes. Yes, I was wearing the flip flops from that certain Hollywood Rite-Aid. And don't forget the pajama bottoms.

My remark about complaining to *International Vogue* should have cut him dead and made him and his tweed rompers slink away.

Instead, he raised an eyebrow, looked me slowly over, from Rite Aid flip flops to PJ bottoms, to stained tee-shirt, to hairiness, and said, "I *work* at *International Vogue*." And he laughed.

43

What were my options? All I could do was put my nose in the air like *International Vogue* is the tackiest rag *no one* ever reads, and sip my latte.

Never had my acting talents come forth so strongly.

Rosalind Barden's short fiction has appeared in print anthologies, including CERN Zoo, *part of the award-winning* Nemonymous *series, and in webzines, such as the UK's late, great* Whispers Of Wickedness. *She wrote and illustrated the children's book* TV Monster. *Her fiction has placed in numerous competitions, including the Shriekfest Film Festival. Her darkly humorous e-novel* American Witch, *now available on Amazon.com, follows the adventures of society's castoffs in a Hollywood stripped of glamour. She lives in Los Angeles, California. Discover more at RosalindBarden.com.*

THE JESTER AND THE GIRL
BY
SELINA ALANIZ

He just stood there at the corner right in front of the Quick Stop convenient store. He was wearing a Jester spandex costume with the purple Plague Doctor mask. He donned black combat boots with thick gold and green chains. I wasn't sure if he noticed me staring. I wondered what he knew. He turned to me and stared, like he heard me thinking about him. I quickly put my ear buds back in and tried to pretend like I wasn't blatantly gawking at him. I could sense something about him. Something...strange. I continued on my way and gave a quick glance back. He was still staring, but this time he had his head a bit tilted to his right side with a big grin across his face.

"Where have you been? You kind of look like shit," Kat said as she gave me a side glance.
"I was out running. Have to make sure my stamina is ready for our Mardi Gras outing as usual," I responded as I dropped my phone onto the kitchen table.
"Yeah, but you look more tired than usual. Wait, you didn't go see him, did you?"
I hated it when Kat brought him up. "No I didn't, but even if I did it doesn't freaking matter because it's not really anyone's business."
She looked at me with her judgmental brown eyes. She was all about finding the one and finding the right guy. I was about not committing. Dale was my non-commitment boyfriend but as of late, things seemed complicated with him. Kat had

45

given me a lecture about his feelings being involved so I had to either dump him or try out the whole relationship thing. I, of course, decided to cut ties.

"Jordan," she said as I began rubbing my temples knowing a lecture was about to ensue, "You promised you would behave so I just need to know that you are."

"I am," I said as I rolled my eyes.

"Okay, so then where were you, really?"

I looked out the window as I sat down on the chair in front of Kat. I felt of a sense of guilt come over me. I didn't want to tell her where I was. I was afraid that she wouldn't understand. We met 9 months ago just after she moved to New Orleans and despite our very different personalities became friends. Roommates seemed the natural next step. I finally came out of my daze. "I told you, I was running."

"Fine. Well it's 9 o' clock in the a.m. so let's get primped and get to the fiestas," she said as she washed her empty cereal bowl.

"Ole," I laughed.

"Two bodies were found this morning. One in a dumpster behind Bob's Grill and another just outside of the city. Police have not commented on whether they are related. We will update you as more information becomes available. Mardi Gras will come to an end tonight and New Orleans is ready to go..."

"Whoa, Jordy, did you hear that? The news said two bodies were found this morning."

I poked my head out of my room to answer. "What? *Two* bodies? What the hell. The day just started and we're already down two people." I could hear the news anchor on the TV talking about Mardi Gras and all the festivities that were happening today as I finished up my makeup. Two bodies, that was perplexing.

"Hey, you ready?" Kat asked.

"Wow, look at you. Sexin' it up, I see," I teased looking at her ensemble: a tight black mini dress that hugged her model-like frame with red high heels and her blonde curly hair neatly surrounding her face. I opted for tight blue jeans, a grey spaghetti

46

strap top, and a thin black sweater. My brown hair was straightened and up in a ponytail. I was a foot shorter than her. I felt like I was simpler looking with my small frame. Kat always seemed to be runway ready with her tanned skin and perfectly round face. People sometimes told me I looked sick because my complexion was light. I never seemed to tan even though I tried numerous times.

"Well I'm gonna find me a man today," she answered.

"Right and I'm going to find me someone who will buy me drinks and..."

"Hey, watch it there, sister. Remember you are behaving."

"But it's Mardi Gras! Now's the time to misbehave," I whined as I hugged her.

"Oh Jordy, I love you too."

Kat stood in front of the mirror we hung by the front door for one last outfit check. I stood beside her to double check mine. I could see my deep blue eyes staring right back at me. We were both 24 years old, but my eyes had seen so much that I felt like I had lived for ages.

"Perfect," Kat said, snapping me out of my own thoughts. We grabbed our bags, masks, and beads and headed out the door. "You know I can't stop thinking about those two bodies they found. I know this isn't the first time or the last but it still gets to me. Why would anyone do that?" she asked looking at me with concern.

I paused for a few moments and then hugged her. I knew that would bring her comfort.

"Let's go to Lyla's first. We can get some shots and then those orange juice drink thingies," Kat suggested.

We walked down Bourbon Street with the rest of New Orleans. We bobbed and weaved our way through people with costumes and masks. I loved Mardi Gras. It was the one time we could be anyone we wanted without being judged. We could act crazy and not worry about what others were saying because they were doing the exact same thing.

Lyla's was packed as to be expected. There was a sea of different colored masks decorated with glitter and feathers seated throughout the bar. Laughter echoed into my ears as we searched for a place to sit.

I never laughed much until I met Kat. I was a product of New Orleans. I was born and raised in the city by my single mother. Our relationship was minimal and almost nonexistent. Instead of bonding like normal families, she hurled insults at me. She'd called me mousy and boring among other things. I hated it so much. She could never give me the one thing I always wanted: love. It didn't matter because she wasn't a factor in my life anymore. If she could only see me now.

Kat described herself as loud and bubbly growing up. She was also bossy and overbearing at times even though she'd deny it, yet we still connected. She was my best friend and gave me what my own mother couldn't.

Two fraternity-looking guys approached and offered to buy us drinks. It took me all of two seconds to say yes. I wasn't looking for a Mr. Right; I just wanted drinks and a good time. After an hour, Kat was already drooling over Maroon; at least that's what I called him. He was wearing a t-shirt with the word "Player" in big bold letters and it was a deep maroon color. I never caught his name and I really didn't care to know it. Kat was strange to me. She constantly preached about finding "the one", yet she was always the first to pick up a guy.

The bar was jam-packed and customers were elbow to elbow. My eyes gazed around the bar. So many people. My heartbeat was fast and I could see my environment begin to move. I needed some fresh air. "Hey, I'm going for a walk. Just take your time and I'll catch up with you later."

Kat gave me that stare that she always gave when she disapproved. "We are supposed to stick together, remember?"

"Well you can stick with him for a while. Clearly you're enjoying his company," I answered with a smile.

"Fine, but don't go too far. Keep your phone handy. And don't go see you-know-who."

I laughed while trying to hide guilt. "I know, I know." I paid the bartender and walked out of the bar, leaving Kat with Maroon.

My hands buttoned the small squared-shape white buttons on my sweater. A sense of calmness and excitement was making its way into me. Shit. I could feel my phone buzzing in my jean back pocket. I was in the middle of something great. What a waste. "Hello, Kat. I'm fine, so calm down please."

"Where are you?! I've been calling and you never freaking answered. What are you doing? You seem out of breath," she said.

"Ugh! Kat, you're not my mom!"

"Oh my God. You're with him aren't you?"

"No," I answered as I stopped and turned to look at the familiar building I had just exited.

"Ok, then you *were* with him. You know Jordy, I am worried about you. This type of relationship isn't normal. You sleep with him whenever you want, and then complain about it when you say he's getting too weepy and clingy. I can't deal with it anymore."

I felt a pang of guilt. Crap. I hated feeling this way. She could always tell when I was lying about something. I wanted to feel alive today. It was Mardi Gras and I couldn't because my best friend decided it was time to harp about my love life. "I'm sorry, Kat. I'll try to do better, okay? Please, I don't want to fight today. Where are you so I can meet up?"

There was a brief silence on the other end of the phone. I could feel frustration set in but I had to stay calm. "Kat?" I asked. For a moment, I thought she had hung up.

"I'm outside of Lyla's," she finally answered.

"I'll be there soon." I hung up and kept walking. I passed people laughing and hugging and families holding hands. Today was my day. Nothing was going to ruin it.

"Okay, where to next?" Kat asked as we walked down the street bumping into beaded and masked people.

"I'm kind of hungry, so let's go to Rudy's," I answered as my stomach started to growl. All I had was alcohol in my system and my stomach was not happy about that.

As we made our way through hordes of people, I glanced across the street. Music was blaring from all the bars and restaurants. I noticed a group of jesters dancing around and interacting with the crowd, but then something else caught my eye. There in the group was a person wearing a purple and green spandex suit. Their black combat boots were decked with gold and green chains. It was a man: tall, muscular. His face was covered with a purple Plague Doctor mask. Then, I had a realization--it was the same man from this morning. I could recognize him, especially with those boots. The nose of the mask was long and pointed. The mask itself was bordered with purple glitter. I found myself staring at the stranger for the second time today. And once again, he noticed me. He stopped and looked at me for few seconds. My eyes made their way to the side of his leg covered in the green spandex. A dark stain. It looked like blood but I couldn't be sure. He saw where my eyes were glaring and looked down to his leg. He looked up again at me, and smiled.

Rudy's was just as packed as Lyla's. Colorful costumes and shirts filled the restaurant just like the bar. I tried to stop thinking about the man and I didn't want Kat to know what I had seen. We finally found seats next to the TV after scouring the restaurant. It was a large room with picnic style tables decorated with small masks. Streamers and banners hung from the ceilings and walls. I wished Mardi Gras was all year round.

"You okay?" Kat asked in her "don't lie to me" tone.

"Yup. Just excited about today. I hope you're enjoying your first Mardi Gras season. Sad that today's the last day," I said with the biggest smile I could muster.

"Yeah, it's quite the experience. I mean this is the time that everyone can be...eccentric," she laughed. "And not be judged. I mean just look around!"

I could tell she was truly enjoying herself. "Nebraska never had something quite like this, huh?"

"Uh no, not exactly," she responded.

We both laughed. Kat was a small town girl looking for a big city to answer her prayers. She found it in New Orleans.

As we waited for our food to arrive, the breaking news graphic appeared on the TV.

"Police discovered another body about an hour ago. The body was found in a dumpster on the 5th block of Canal Street. Officials believe it may be connected to at least one of the bodies found earlier this morning. Police have now officially confirmed that one of the bodies found this morning was wearing a purple mask. The body that was recently found also had a purple mask. Police are hesitant to call it a serial killer's work. No word on the body found outside of the city and its connection to these murders. We will update you as we get more information."

"Wow, three bodies in a span of a day? A serial killer? What the hell is going on?" Kat asked as water welled in her eyes.

I could see fear in her face. I didn't know what to tell her. Despite that, I was her best friend and it was my job to be there for her. I looked into her worried eyes and said the one thing that would bring her comfort. "We'll be okay. We just need to stick together, and we'll be fine." She grabbed my hand and held it until the waitress brought out our food.

I looked into the large, round mirror in the ladies room. I couldn't help but feel a bit annoyed and angry, but Kat couldn't know that. She would never understand.

I began thinking about the two bodies that were connected by a mask. A purple mask. The other body was like a forgotten memory that no one really cared to remember. That body was a somebody. They were a person, too. But no one cared because they weren't wearing a mask? I shook my head as tears filled my eyes. I had to calm down. I couldn't let Kat see me like this. I looked at my image again in the mirror and took a few deep breaths. My body began to relax.

My mind began to wonder to the man in the spandex suit. He was wearing a purple mask. He had a dark stain that may have been blood. Could he be the supposed serial killer they were looking for? Maybe he was. Or maybe I was just reading too much into it. A girl wearing a Mardi Gras NOLA shirt stumbled into the bathroom laughing. She looked like she didn't have a care in the world. I wondered what that felt like.

51

Due to technical difficulties, as the Mayor put it, the parade started after 7:00 pm. Kat and I had spent the rest of the afternoon in and out of shops. As usual, Kat did the most damage and had to lug around six bags. I walked out with one key chain in my pocket. I was never much of a shopper, but Kat was the complete opposite. Now, we were finally able to watch the parade. Floats of all shapes and sizes drove down the street. High school bands marched in their uniforms. Others dressed in Mardi Gras fashion flooded the sidewalks. I looked at Kat and could see she was enthralled. She acted like we were at Disneyworld. I was happy my best friend was experiencing this with me.

Just as my eyes made their way back to the parade, I saw him on the other side of the street. It was the same Jester man from earlier. His body was still, almost like a statue. Despite the distractions of floats, people and music, I knew he was looking at me. He turned around and walked into the alley behind him. It was an invitation.

"Hey, I see Dale. I think I need to talk to him about some stuff," I lied.

"Jordy, you already had action for the day with him. What more can you possibly say?" She was annoyed. Her voice was high. Her eyes were glued to the parade.

"It's complicated, Kat, okay? I'll see you in a bit."

"What happened to experiencing this together and sticking together?" she muttered as her face intentionally stayed looking in the other direction.

At this point, I didn't care if she was mad at me. "Just chill out, Kat. I'll see you later." I walked off not looking back. He was waiting for me.

Despite the dark evening sky blanketing New Orleans, there were lights on all over town. The parade provided enough light for me to see my way through the alley. What was I doing? Why was I following a spandex wearing possible psychopath? Deep down I knew why.

I slowly made my way around corners careful not to make too much noise. He knew I was coming and didn't want to give him time to react when I did find him.

Purple in my side view. I turned to the right. He was standing at the entrance of a building. It was dark but I could make out some of the letters on the building. The word METAL was painted in white.

He disappeared quickly into the darkness of the building. I ran to the entrance and pulled out my phone to use as a flashlight. The parade lights failed to shine inside the dingy building. I used the soft light of my phone to try and make out the room I was in. There were broken pipes and shards of glass littered all over the floor. I could hear the squeaks of rats somewhere in the room. Where was he? I walked over to the windows. At least some moonlight streamed in enough for me to see a bit more. My concentration was broken when a deep voice rumbled in the empty room.

"Hi there. I figured you'd come."

I tried to find him in the darkness. "Why don't you come to the light so I can see you better?" I said sternly. Purple and green made their way to the light. He wasn't wearing his mask. I could finally see him fully. He was tanned, with short, black, curly hair and piercing dark eyes. His nose was long and prominent. He was actually quite handsome. His spandex suit was tight to his body. His physique reminded me of a Greek god statue. If circumstances were different, we'd be doing something else right at this moment. A bright glare suddenly broke my gaze. It was a knife. He was holding it with his right hand while his left hand held his mask. "It was you, wasn't it? The bodies with the masks?"

He laughed at me like I had told him some hilarious joke. "What do you think? You knew from the moment you saw me this morning; I knew you were different. You studied me like you recognized me. Yet you had no idea what I actually looked like. How?"

I smiled. "Let's just say I'm really good at reading people like you."

His deep laugh grumbled throughout the empty building. "You're a funny girl. Too bad we couldn't get to know each other better. Perhaps another time or place, we would have been friends. Don't you agree?"

I didn't say anything. I was doing my best to keep my cool. I needed a weapon, and fast. Broken shards of glass were spread out on the floor. I just needed to be quick enough to grab one. "Well, if you're going to gut me, maybe we can do a little something to please me first?" I walked slowly over to him careful not to lose his gaze. I made my way to him and as I got closer, I could see his face staring at me with anticipation. I stood in front about a foot shorter than him. Our eyes never wavered from each other. I knew the knife was only inches from me. His head slowly bent down to kiss me. Just as our lips met, my hand met his throat with a quick blow. He dropped the knife and fell back while he choked. His hands were grasping his throat. I picked up the knife and jammed it into his thigh. He screamed in pain and held his leg as it bled. The anger that I had managed to push back suddenly heaved up like an angry wave. I grabbed a shard of glass and jammed it into his other thigh. His screams got louder and I became more annoyed.   He did his best to hold on to the two holes in his legs. Crimson red liquid. I loved that color. "Shut up," I whispered. He didn't.

"Shut up," I said louder. He continued whimpering.

"Shut up!" I slapped him across his face. I felt the burning sensation work itself throughout my hand. He stopped and looked at me in shock. He looked confused.

"You crazy bi-" he started.

"Enough," I said as I grabbed his chin. "It's my turn now." I got up and walked around to make sure no one else was around. I walked to the broken window where the moonlight was coming through. "You know today was supposed to be a great day for me. It was supposed to be my day. My day," I emphasized. "But you had to go and screw everything up. You and your stupid bodies and your stupid masks. I mean seriously? That's not even original!" I yelled into the darkness. I turned around and walked to him and sat down next to him. "I had everything planned just like always. And for what?"

54

He finally spoke. "You're just like me, aren't you?"

I was silent.

He continued. "The other body outside of the city. That was you, wasn't it?"

I just stared into the darkness as his voice rumbled around me. I could feel the warm tears fall down my cheeks. I wiped them away with my bloody hand. "Mardi Gras is so much fun," I finally answered. "It's meant for people to release the self that they only dream about. You get to be whoever you want. You get to celebrate and not be judged. That's why I do what I do during this time. Once a year I get to be who I want and do what I want. Just once a year. And I get recognized for it." I looked to my side and he was glaring at me. It felt like he was almost insisting I go on with my story. "Every Mardi Gras for the past four years I get to take what I want," I went on.

"And what's that?" he asked.

I drew my face closer to his because I wanted to make sure he heard me. "Life." I could hear myself laugh a little. "There's another body, you know. He's on Oak Street just waiting to be discovered. But your stunt came along and just stole his limelight. My limelight."

"Why do you do it? Everyone's got a story," he asked me.

He was beginning to squirm a bit. I grabbed another shard of glass and plunged it into his left side. He howled in pain once again.

I answered him. "I do it because I like it." I smiled at him. He was so attractive. Wrong place, wrong time. "Do you want to know a secret?" I asked him. "I'm going to tell you something I've never told anyone else. You want to know who my first victim was?" I paused to see if he was still conscious.

He looked at me with intrigue. "Who?" he finally answered.

I looked up at the ceiling and noticed bird nests. The chicks in those eggs were lucky. They had families. "My mother," I answered.

It was quiet for what seemed like eternity.

The Jester broke the solemn silence. "Well aren't we quite a pair. The Jester and the girl," he laughed. "You saw me this morning, and then again this afternoon. You didn't know me, yet you recognized me. You know why?" he said as he slowly picked up his hand and touched my cheek, "Because you *are* me."

I felt the rumbling in my core and the anger explode again. I picked up another shard. I lowered my head to his and lightly kissed him on the lips. "I am not you... I am better than you." I pushed the glass into his forehead and watched as the life left his eyes.

"You lied, Jordy. You just left me there alone and never came back."

Kat was angry with me as she should be. I was a horrible friend to her today. "I'm sorry, Kat. I really am. Things just came up but I should have called. I am so sorry. Please don't be mad."

Kat looked at me from across our table. "I bet Dale had a great time," she said as she rolled her eyes.

I laughed. "Forgive me?" I asked.

"I suppose. Only because I love you." she smiled. "I guess my first Mardi Gras is in the books," she said as she got up from our kitchen table.

"Hey," I said. "I promise next year will be better." Kat laughed and went to her room. I walked to mine and looked at myself in the mirror. "Much better. Much, much better."

Selina Alaniz was born and raised in the Rio Grande Valley located in southern Texas where she currently resides with her family. She graduated with a bachelor's degree in Communication- Journalism. She has a dog that loves to give hugs and a cat that may be planning world domination. She loves couponing and will talk about it to anyone who will listen. Cooking, watching horror movies and reading horror novels are other hobbies she partakes in when she isn't scouring for coupons. Selina is a newcomer to the writing world. "The Jester and the Girl" is her first published short story.

LORD OF THE PEACOCKS
BY
GWEN MAYO

"Yes sir, there's no doubt about it. She's been murdered."

Chief Johnson swore. "Sorry, Bob. Seal off the crime scene. Keep everybody in the lodge. I'll get there as quick as I can,"

"What's wrong?" his wife asked as he climbed out of bed.

"Mardi Gras, Maggie," he grumbled. "Nobody in town ever gave Mardi Gras a thought until Katrina flooded New Orleans. Now the whole county goes plumb crazy once a year."

Maggie Johnson brushed the hair back from her face. "There's no need to get all riled up about it, Sam. I know it makes a lot of extra work for you, but the celebration brings needed money into town. City Council isn't going to change its mind about allowing the revelry." She gave him a sympathetic kiss on the cheek. "Which ball got out of hand this year?"

"I wish it were drunken partiers," he said. "I'd like to give Reverend Wilks a stiff kick in the rear. He's the one who suggested we use the money from our missions offering to host a community-wide hurricane relief event. This festival started with his block party. That wasn't anywhere near Mardi Gras. But once the city council saw how much money a New Orleans-themed party raised, they were certain a Tannersville Mardi Gras would pull in tourists."

"Now Sam, you can't blame the preacher for your troubles. We helped a lot of people with that party and it didn't cost much. Tim Crider knew a jazz band that was willing to donate their time to a good cause. Miss Mabel talked to her women's club about cookin' up some Cajun food. Besides, your department pitched in too. I have pictures to prove you're as guilty as the rest of Tannersville in getting Mardi Gras started here."

"That was supposed to be a one-time event, in the middle of summer," he snapped. "I had no part in turning this town into a Bourbon Street nightmare once a year. A woman's been murdered, Maggie. *Murdered.* The krewes, the parties, the drinking, and the crime aren't just down in New Orleans anymore. They are right here in Tannersville."

"Murder, here? Surely not. There hasn't been a murder in Tannersville since...I can't remember when."

"Well you can start counting from today," he said. "Some fool rammed a peacock feather through a woman's ear."

Driving across town, Chief Johnson regretted the shock he'd given his wife. It wasn't her fault that the fundraiser had been allowed to turn into a week-long drunken orgy. Most of the fault could be laid squarely at the feet of the city council. He had argued until he was blue in the face, but all they saw was the money that rolled into town. First, they voted to allow the selling and drinking of beer on the street during the festival. When he had to start arresting girls for indecent exposure, they suspended those laws for the week. Two years ago they started giving awards and official recognition to the Lord and Lady of each krewe. It was unbelievable what some folks would do for a trophy and the prime seat on a parade float.

Now the newly crowned Lady Mischief from the Peacock Krewe was dead. It was up to him to figure out why. The same council members who started this mess would be screaming for him to solve the crime before it cast a shadow over the town's big event.

"Bloody politicians," he said, pounding his fist against the steering wheel. "And a feather—who kills a person with a feather?"

Chief Johnson couldn't fathom how anyone could ram a feather into someone's ear hard enough to kill. What kind of sick mind would a plan like that take root in? It had to be planned.

Nobody got into a fight and grabbed a feather to use as a weapon.

He was so busy trying to wrap his mind around the crime, that he forgot that the parade floats were all being driven into place at the north end of town. There was a rude reminder when he rounded the bend onto River Road and nearly hit a two story riverboat head on. Chief Johnson swerved to miss the float, only to sideswipe a green dragon parked on the shoulder of the road.

He got out of the car and looked the damage over. One side of the metallic green skirting was ripped loose from the dragon's body, but there was no harm to the flatbed trailer supporting the gaudy beast. Its krewe was going to have to do little more than staple the bunting back into place. They would have plenty of time to fix the float after they wrapped up their Mardi Gras Eve Ball. That is, if anyone was still sober enough to hold a staple gun.

His cruiser hadn't fared as well. The right quarter panel looked like an accordion and one headlight was busted. He was relieved that the damage was mostly cosmetic. At least it was drivable. He told the float driver to stop by the station for a copy of the accident report after the parade. There would be time enough then to discuss damages.

Bob Little, the officer who called him, was waiting by the ambulance at the front door of the Moose Lodge when he arrived. "What happened to your car?" he said.

"Later," the chief said. "Right now I want you to bring me up to date on this catastrophe."

Officer Little shook his head. "It's the damnedest thing I've ever seen, Chief. She's just lying on one of the couches. You'd think she was sleeping if it weren't for a yard long peacock feather hanging out the side of her head."

"That's really what killed her? Are you sure there's no other injuries?"

"Not that I could see, Chief." Officer Little pointed to the large gray van pulling into the parking lot. "Looks like the state mobile crime lab is here. Dr. Roark will be glad to hear that. He's been waiting for you and them in the lounge. Nothing's been moved."

The chief took a deep breath. "Are all the guests accounted for?"

"Everybody invited and their guests. Staff too. The security guard says nobody got in without an invitation."

"Good work, Bob. Do we have a positive identification of the body?"

Officer Little's eyes grew wide. "Didn't I tell you? Its Mayor Gentry's wife, Carol. The mayor's fit to be tied. He's been making all sorts of threats against us, well, mostly you."

"Any accusations flying around?"

"Plenty. The Gentrys changed krewes this year. They've been part of the Eagles. It caused some hard feelings when she ran for queen her first year in this krewe."

"Who's most offended by the Gentrys changing krewes?"

"Well," Officer Little began, "Brenda Bailey been Lady Mischief five years running. Her husband isn't thrilled either; those commercials he runs with her in the parade getup won't work this year. Then there's the mayor. He was arguing with Carol earlier. Nobody admits knowing what the fight was about."

"That gives us somewhere to start. Has anyone tried to leave?"

"Lots of complaints, but nobody tried to force their way out."

"Who's complaining the loudest?"

"The smokers," Officer Little said. "We're lucky the fire truck and EMT's arrived together. They've tripped the fire alarm three times. One of them opened the men's room window to try to clear the smoke, but that tripped a different alarm."

"Who called us?"

"The Mayor."

"Thanks Bob," he said, reaching for the door. "Start checking contact information and arranging for statements. I would like to talk to Mayor Gentry and the Baileys. Hang on to them, but we'll get the rest of these folks out of here when I finish with the doctor."

Mayor Gentry hardly gave him a chance to step inside. His pudgy finger was inches from the chief's face as he unleashed his anger. There was a large dose of fear and grief mixed with the barrage of accusations Gentry heaped on the Chief. The mayor's bulldog face was half hidden by his mask, making it difficult to tell if the grief was genuine. Nothing could mask the fear. In that, the mayor was not alone; frightened people crowded around him. Questions peppered him from all sides.

Chief Johnson tried to be reassuring, but in a sea of glittering costumes and frightened people it was disorienting. He couldn't blame them for being frightened. The killer was probably still in the room. He wasn't going to be able to figure out who that person was if he had to stand here all night answering their questions. It was a welcome relief when two officers pushed through the crowd and cleared a path for him.

Dr. Roark didn't look up when the chief stepped through the door into the lodge's lounge. "About time you got here, Chief."

"Had a little accident on the way over."

The doctor gave him a cursory glance. "You seem to have come through it without a scratch."

"Mrs. Gentry wasn't as lucky. What can you tell me about her death?"

"Homicide. A single stab wound through the left cochlea. The body was discovered almost immediately. She can't have been dead for more than a few minutes when the mayor found her. The body is still warm." The doctor paused a second or two. "I can't be certain of this, but it wouldn't surprise me if your killer had some military or martial arts training."

"What makes you think that?"

Dr. Roark picked up a long plastic evidence bag and handed it to the chief. "See the way the shaft has splintered? In a single blow, your killer drove that into her left ear with enough force to go through the brain and strike the skull on the opposite side of her head. You couldn't just stick the feather in her ear with a push to achieve this amount of damage. The precision of the blow indicates skill. The condition of the murder weapon suggests that you're looking for a man in good physical condition."

The chief winced.

"If it makes you feel better, Mrs. Gentry probably didn't know what happened to her. I'll need a toxicology report to confirm it, but odds are she was unconscious at the time of death."

"That kind of begs the question, doesn't it?"

"What's that, Chief?"

"He's standing over an unconscious woman. Why bother with the feather? A strong man could have snapped her neck. He wouldn't even need to be strong to suffocate her. If he had done something like that, it might have been hours before anyone noticed she was dead."

"I see your point." The doctor said. "You would have to be pretty drunk not to notice this thing hanging out of her ear. Leaving the feather assured rapid discovery. "

"That's the way I see it," the chief said. He couldn't have made a murder more obvious. "Anyway, Doc, the state mobile crime lab pulled in about the time I did. Is it all right to let the crime scene investigators in?"

"Nothing more I can do here," the doctor said. "I'll let you know what I find at autopsy."

The chief studied the scene a few minutes. Bob Little had been right when he said that she looked like she was sleeping. Her gold evening bag lay on the table in front of her. He slipped on disposable gloves and examined its contents: a lipstick, a mirrored compact, her car keys, her driver's license, and a single credit card. The glittering little bag reminded him of half a dozen his wife had owned over the twenty-six years they had been married. "Just the necessities," he could almost hear Maggie say. She was going to take it hard when she learned that Carol was the victim. They had been friends since high school.

He took out his camera and snapped a couple of pictures before dialing Bob Little's number. There would be dozens of photographs from the crime scene team, but those would come later. He didn't want to wait for a backed-up state crime lab to process his murder case. The mayor and the press wouldn't be harassing them. Besides, if Bob was right, his killer was still on the premises. There were only two doors to this room. The one he

62

entered came from the lodge hall.

"Dr. Roark's ready to turn the room over to the crime scene team, Bob," he said, as he tested the other door. "When the state team gives the okay, have the EMT's transport the body to the morgue. Also, there is a door here that leads to a hallway across from the restrooms. Have the CSI's examine the area. Our killer could have gotten out this way."

Chief Johnson started to hang up when something else came to mind. "Bob, where's Carol's crown?"

"What?"

"Lady Mischief and Lord Mayhem rule the ball and the float. As I recall, they both have elaborate gold-plated crowns decorated with peacock feathers," the chief explained. "Her crown isn't here. Have you seen it?"

"No, sir."

"Ask the mayor," the chief ordered. "I want to know what happened to that crown. And find out who Lord Mayhem is this year. Then get his crown and bag it. If I recall correctly, his has a row of tall feathers across the front, just like the one that killed Mrs. Gentry."

"Will do, Chief, but you know that will cause a ruckus."

"I know," the chief said. "It can't be helped."

"Anything else?"

"Yes. I want their feathered capes, too. Parade or no parade, this is a murder investigation. They will just have to do without peacock feathers. And Bob, hold on to Lord Mayhem for questioning. If there's a single feather missing from his costume, I want a good explanation."

Rounding up the Baileys and Mayor Gentry wasn't hard. The three of them were standing together near the front door. Officer Little took them to the small room Chief Johnson was using as a makeshift office.

"Thanks Bob," the chief said. "Have you located those crowns yet?"

The young officer's neck reddened. The search for Lord Mayhem and the missing regalia hadn't gone well. "The only Mardi Gras stuff we found was a bunch of beads in the storage closet. Security is adamant that Lord Mayhem hasn't left, but nobody can locate him. We're still searching the building for him and the stuff you want."

Chief Sam Johnson was silent for a long moment. His dark eyes moved slowly over the faces of the Peacock Krewe members gathered in front of him. They came to rest on the mayor. "Just who and where is Lord Mayhem?" he asked.

"Owen Hale," Mayor Gentry said. "I'm sure he's around here somewhere."

The chief's brows shot up. "You joined the same crew as the man who's run against you in the last three elections?"

"Nothing would suit Carol but us joining this krewe. She's been trying to be the lady of one of the krewes since we started holding the festival. Some of her friends convinced her that she could win the title if we joined the Peacocks." His voice softened. "I guess they were right, but she never got to enjoy her victory."

"Is that what you were arguing about?"

Mayor Gentry's face turned as white as his mask. "I—that is, we were not fighting. We just disagreed about the way Owen was hanging all over her. He's never gotten over the fact she married me instead of him."

"Well," Mrs. Bailey said. "You wouldn't have had to worry about that if you'd stayed with your regular krewe. But no, you had to horn in on ours."

"Good grief, Brenda, give it a rest," her husband said. "She's dead. That stupid crown doesn't matter now."

Brenda's hands clutched her hips. "And whose fault is that? The mayor admits they were fighting. He killed her himself."

Chief Johnson cleared his throat. "Do you have evidence to support that accusation, Mrs. Bailey?"

"Umm—I..." she stammered.

"Of course she doesn't," Mayor Gentry shouted. "It's pure slander."

She glared at her husband. "Michael, are you going to let him talk to me that way?"

Michael Bailey staggered over and sat down in one of the wooden chairs the chief had procured for his interviews. "Tell me something, Chief; do you have any idea who really killed her?"

"Michael!"

"I told you to give it a rest, Brenda. Mayor Gentry isn't any more capable of killing Carol that way than you are." He wagged his index finger in her direction, and giggled like a naughty school boy. "You would have liked to though, wouldn't you Brenda?"

"So would you. Shooting those new commercials is going to cost you a pretty penny. That's what you really care about, isn't it Michael? Your true love has always been your bank account."

"You're pretty fond of it yourself, Brenda; at least you're fond of spending my money," her husband said.

Chief Johnson had listened to all he could stand. "Do any of you have anything useful to add to this investigation?"

Three blank stares answered him.

"How about Owen? When did Lord Mayhem last put in an appearance?"

Michael Bailey snorted. "He put in a fine appearance to kick off the ball, didn't he, Mayor?"

"You're drunk, Bailey," Gentry said.

"So was your wife, Mayor. Drunk and up to some mischief with his lordship. Those two were all over each other the way they used to be in high school. The last I saw of either of them was around midnight, Chief. They tangled together like love-struck teenagers when they stumbled into the lounge."

Mayor Gentry lunged at him. "You take that back, Bailey," he shouted, grabbing him around the neck. "You're not going to drag my wife's good name through the mud."

Officer Little pulled the mayor off before he could do any serious harm.

"You both saw it," Brenda shouted. "He tried to kill my husband. Arrest him!"

"I will Mrs. Bailey, and you *and* your husband," the chief said. "Bob, have one of the boys out there lock these three up until I get to the bottom of this. Then you and I are going to search this building until we find Owen Hale or prove beyond any shadow of a doubt that he did leave. If he did get out of here, I want to know how and why."

"You can't arrest me. I'm the mayor."

Chief Johnson clenched and unclenched his teeth as he tried to fight back his temper. Then he turned to face the mayor.

"Mister Mayor," he said in the tone he usually reserved for those times when his children tried his patience beyond the limit, "nobody is above the law, not even you. Officer Little pulled you off Mr. Bailey before you choked him to death, but assault is still a crime. If you go along quietly, I will consider just leveling assault charges instead of booking you for attempted murder."

The portion of the mayor's face that was visible under his mask turned beet red. He opened his mouth, sputtered, then turned and left the room.

"Would you come with me, Mrs. Bailey, Mr. Bailey?" Officer Little asked.

Brenda Bailey started to protest, but changed her mind when she got a look at Chief Johnson's face. Bailey tried to cooperate, but the full effect of his drinking when he tried to get out of his chair. Only Officer Little's timely intervention prevented Michael Bailey from landing face down on the concrete floor. He clung to the young policeman as they left.

Chief Johnson sighed, closed the door, and picked up his phone. The time flashed 3:26 a.m. when his screen woke. He'd been at the lodge for more than two hours and still didn't have a firm grasp of what had happened. If Michael Bailey was right about the time, Owen Hale was with Mrs. Gentry near the time of her death. Where was Hale?

He started to punch in the number for the station house, then changed his mind. Before he issued a BOLO he needed to know what officers should be on the lookout for. He needed to see if Owen Hale's truck was still in the parking lot.

One look out the front door of the lodge confirmed that the truck was still parked beside the lodge. He went outside to have a look in the windows. They would have to get a search warrant to do more than take a quick look, unless potential evidence was in plain sight.

There wasn't exactly evidence of murder inside Hale's truck. Chief Johnson blinked and reached for his flashlight.

"Over here, Bob," he shouted, as he aimed the light through the driver's side window.

Chief Johnson was thankful that the vehicle's lone passenger couldn't see the expression on his face as the beam of his light moved slowly over the floorboard of the truck. Until that moment, he thought he'd see about every predicament a person could get into. Nothing prepared him for the sight of Owen Hale lying on the floor of his truck, trussed up like a Thanksgiving turkey, and wearing nothing but duct tape and his boxers.

"I think I saw him move," the chief said, handing his keys to Officer Little. "There's a Slim Jim under the front seat of my car."

Chief Johnson was on the phone with the paramedics when Little returned. He handed the shiny strip of metal to the chief.

"Thanks, Bob." the chief said, as he hung up. "Get this area cordoned off, then have one of the CSI's get out here."

The chief considered it lucky for Hale that he drove a vintage Ford Ranger, one built when the Rangers were full sized pickups, and that the locks were still the button type. If the vehicle were newer, he would have had to break the window to get inside. There was an audible click as he popped the driver's side lock. Hale was scrunched into the floor in a fetal position, unconscious but still breathing. His skin indicated that he was in the early stages of exposure. No doubt Hale had been in this position for quite a while, but how long? Party security was certain that Hale was there when they checked ID's. The chief snapped a couple of close-up photographs with his camera phone before taking his knife out and cutting through the duct tape bindings on his hands and feet.

Hale roused enough to moan a time or two before the paramedics arrived, but not enough to question. The chief stepped out of the way and let the emergency medical team do their job. As soon as the EMT's lifted Owen Hale out of the truck, crime scene tape closed off the area.

The Channel Four news van arrived as the ambulance pulled away.

"Just what we need," Officer Little grumbled. "Did you

see the way those guys had to swerve to miss the ambulance?"

"Yes, I did, Bob," the chief said, his eyes following the taillights of the ambulance until it vanished around the bend. "Call the station and have them send an officer to the hospital to guard Hale."

"You think someone will try to get to him?" Bob Little couldn't help noticing that his face wore the same distant expression that his boss always got when he was remembering some detail the rest of the force hadn't caught.

"Chief? Do you think Mr. Hale is in danger?"

"More danger than he realizes, Bob. Would you mind taking over here? I need to reach Judge Andrews and get a search warrant."

The chief hadn't waited for an answer. He was sprinting for his cruiser with the camera crew close behind him. Seconds later, the flashing lights of the chief's car cast a blue tinge on the cloud of dust blowing in his wake.

Judge Andrews wasn't happy to be awakened in the wee hours of the morning, but after listening to what Chief Johnson had to say, he agreed to a limited search of the Peacocks' float.

Dawn was breaking over the Mississippi River when the chief got back to River Road. He parked opposite the huge riverboat responsible for the damage to his car. The search warrant was in his hand when he banged on the door of the Peterbilt hidden under layers of glittering gold. Chief Johnson wasn't surprised when no one answered. He knocked again, loud enough to sleepy shouts "I'm trying to sleep here" from the driver of the Dragon Krewe float.

"Sorry," the chief yelled back, "Police business."

He climbed aboard the float and looked for the big plastic sacks of parade loot. If he was right, this was where his proof was hidden. One by one, he dumped the contents of the bags onto the floor of the float. Plastic coins, piles of beads, candy for the children, and finally the capes and crowns tumbled out. Just as he suspected, the feather that killed Carol Gentry had come from Lord Mayhem's crown. He had removed one from the other side to even the appearance, but anyone examining the crown could she there should have been seven, not five, feathers adorning the rim. He bagged and sealed the parade regalia.

There was one more piece of the puzzle needed to make the case fit together. He punched in Bob Little's number as he got in his car.

"Where are you, Chief?" Officer Little asked.

"On my way to the hospital to check on Owen Hale. There's a couple of things I need you to do there, Bob. First, bag those beads you found in the storage closet. I want them checked for fingerprints."

"Will do, Chief."

"As soon as it's light enough, I'd like you to search the woods behind the lodge."

"The woods, Chief? What am I looking for?"

"If I'm right, you are going to find Owen Hale's work clothes and motorcross bike." The chief grinned, wishing he could see Bob Little's face about now. He hung up the phone and started his car.

Owen Hale was stretched out in bed watching the news when Chief Johnson arrived. "Come in, Chief," he said. "I believe I owe you a huge thank-you. They say you're the one who found me."

"I'm sure that someone would have found you by daylight, Owen," the chief said. "Can you tell me what happened?"

"I don't really remember much, Carol said she was feeling funny after the toasts. She wanted to lie down, so I helped her into the lounge. I didn't feel well either. I stepped out for some fresh air. I guess I blacked out. Next thing I remember was the ambulance."

"You're saying the last thing you remember is stepping outside for some fresh air," Chief Johnson said, making a note. His phone rang as he closed the notebook.

"Thanks, Bob. I'll explain later. Have the boys pack it up and go back to their regular duties." The chief shut off his phone and turned back to Owen.

"You and Carol were close once, weren't you Owen?"

"That was a long time ago," he said, eyeing the chief suspiciously. "She married Gentry right after graduation. I joined the Marines. What does that have to do with anything?"

"I think it has everything to do with her death, Owen. I think you are the friend who suggested she join the Peacocks. You helped her become your lady. Maybe you thought that she would leave her husband, or maybe you planned to kill her all along. But you killed her. You took one of the feathers from your crown and jammed it through her ear. Then you took both crowns and left the club to hide the evidence."

"You're crazy," he shouted. "Have you forgotten I was unconscious the whole time?"

"Not the whole time," Chief Johnson said. "Not when you ran me off the road trying to get the float into place for the parade. You weren't unconscious when you rode your motorbike back to the lodge."

Owen paled.

"That's right, Owen. Officer Little just called to confirm that he had found your bike. I found the crowns on the float where you put them. Do you want to know what I think? I think those are your trucks pulling the floats today. I think you arranged to ride with one of your drivers to show up before the parade. You probably told him you would put the float in the lineup for him. You killed Carol. Then you stuck around just long enough for the body to be discovered. You wanted Security to vouch for you."

"You're crazy."

"Am I?" the chief said. "Then we won't find your fingerprints on the beads that you stashed in the supply closet? I already have the crowns you hid on the float in one of the chum bags. What about the window you climbed out? Did you have gloves, or will we find your prints there?"

"Chief, I—I..." he stammered.

"Owen Hale, I'm arresting you for the murder of Carol Gentry," Chief Johnson began...

Gwen Mayo is passionate about blending the colorful history of her native Kentucky with her love for mystery fiction.

She currently lives and writes in Tarpon Springs, Florida, but grew up in a large Irish family in the hills of Eastern Kentucky. Her stories have appeared in anthologies, at online short fiction sites, and in micro-fiction collections.

Circle of Dishonor, *her first novel, is set during the turbulent political upheaval of post-Civil War Kentucky at a time when murder was more common in Kentucky than it was anywhere else in the United States.*

KREWE OF BAYOU BLACK
BY
NATHAN PETTIGREW

I aim for his head, and he has no idea. He doesn't see us—so he's safe for now—he doesn't have to die, and we don't have to call this job a bust just yet. His back turned to us, the cop waits for the parade from a spot on the sidewalk that's dead center in view from between the two buildings where we stand perfectly still.

Our costumes are common eye masks: sequin, satin and feather, whole masks with glitter and face paint—all green, yellow and purple—the colors of Mardi Gras.

I nod, giving the crew the go ahead, surprised to have even seen a cop on foot. This isn't New Orleans. This is somewhere better, a place much smaller where police during Mardi Gras are stretched thin—the thinnest they'll be stretched all year, leaving no better time than now to rob Dupont's Jewelry.

The two-story brick building is like most on Barrow Street, so close together that kids can jump from one balcony to the next during a parade to catch more beads.

Behind Dupont's, we find the door gate pulled up and a crack in the glass of the actual door. It's not closed all the way.

"It's open," our locksmith says, shaking his head at me. "The door's open."

"Go ahead," I tell him, our weapons drawn.

Sticking out on the floor from behind the counter to the left are a man's feet in expensive dress shoes. Mr. Dupont. His face is barely recognizable beneath the wet veil of blood.

Multiple knives are planted in his head through the top, the back, all over.

"Stay here," I tell everyone, heading upstairs and switching off the safety on my firearm. Second floor is dark, a bathroom, and three empty rooms.

"Clear," I yell out, stopping in front of the thin white curtains in the French doors to the balcony that allow me to see the parade, the people, and a slice of life that's truly our own in Terrebonne Parish.

An hour south of New Orleans, Terrebonne's Mardi Gras is more about family and fun, plus food and more food for the Catholics among us who go all out before fasting for Lent. It's about gathering as one.

Where outsiders travel to New Orleans for debauchery, citizens of Terrebonne come out for each other and to celebrate the community of Bayou Black with the only real disruption or unpleasantness coming from the horse manure in the street.

"Don't move," a voice yells out. "Hands on your head."

I know that voice. Detective Anselmo.

Careful, quiet, I peek downstairs and see my crew— Cameron, Buddy, and Blake—lying face down with their hands folded against the backs of their heads.

I book it. Outside on the balcony, looking down, I see the cops guarding the front. I jump back, unseen. I leap to the next balcony over.

Only two kids in the crowd see me, the rest of the herd drawn proper to the parade: the Shriners throwing doubloons and forcing most of the other kids to scatter the streets for the aluminum coins that come in all colors.

I jump to the ground and walk. Cops didn't see my costume. Blending in the rest of the crowd, I have a good chance of escaping but I need to move with the parade and not away from it until some floats have passed and I've caught some beads to take with me. I have to be patient. Every move has to make sense—despite nothing about the raid on Dupont's making even the slightest lick of sense.

Anselmo is one of Mr. Val's. His number one, actually.

A bookie and the biggest fish in the water as far as Bayou Black goes, Val Broussard owns a great deal of local real estate, some restaurants, and a handful of cops on the parish police force who see to it that the old man remains untouchable.

Anselmo would've never moved in without his consent, but even crazier is the fact that I have a dead body on my hands—a life sentence I'll die before serving.

Mr. Val taught me to always have a Plan C because no Plan B was worth the horse manure in the streets without one. Well my Plan C is a storage locker off Highway 311, and inside is a boat, filthy and useless on water, but good to hold some cash, some clothes, and even a couple of suits.

Mr. Val taught me a lot, practically raising me after my mother and father were killed in a head-on collision with a drunk driver during Mardi Gras one year. A member on the board that oversees homes for orphans and troubled youth, he took an interest in me. He gave me a life, and I repaid that debt by giving it back and living for his needs first and foremost—be it odd jobs around his mansion or jobs like the one today involving jewelry stores.

He's also the father of the young woman I love. Angie. My on-again, off-again girlfriend. On sometimes because the love is real. Off again because so is the life I lead.

And with a few quiet minutes to myself, I call her cell.

"Claude," she says, relieved and anxious. "What happened? It's all over the news."

"It wasn't us, Angie. I swear. We found him like that."

"What are you saying?"

"I'm saying we were set up, but I have no idea how or why. Can you get me into the Tableau tonight?"

"Of course I can get you in," she says. "But how is going anywhere near the Tableau a good idea?"

"It's the only way I'll get close to your father. He won't see me on his own. Things are too hot right now. But I gotta see him, Angie. Something's wrong here and I've gotta set things right. Look, I don't need to be there for the whole thing. Just the dance."

"Okay," she says. "I'll text you when the dance starts and meet you out front."

A woman of her word, Angie meets me in front of the auditorium wearing a long green dress that leaves her shoulders and arms exposed, her chest showing through the V cut, and her dirty blonde curls pulled up from the back.

She's stunning.

"Promise you'll be careful," she says.

"Of course," I say.

"No, Claude. Look at me and promise. Don't push it in there."

I squeeze her hand, smiling. "I won't."

Angie smile is all hers—truly unique. Her teeth aren't exactly straight, but not ugly. They're just, they're Angie.

She brings me inside the auditorium where people are indeed dancing, talking, and having a good time.

Like most krewes in Terrebonne Parish, there isn't much color to be found in the faces of this crowd, aside from the purple, yellow and green that some of them wear. Tonight's event, the Tableau, is the part of the season when a carnival krewe announces their king and queen. Dukes and maids are also introduced. A closed ceremony to the general public, members get dressed up--if not in costume, then tuxes and gowns.

Make no mistake. While it all looks and seems like fun, these are the richest of the rich and they take this as seriously as they take their country clubs. It costs money to be a member, money to ride, and money to buy beads. We're talking thousands. The dukes and maids of the king's court are Southern belles who will never work a day in their life, and boys who will never have to worry about coming home with calluses on their hands after a twelve-hour shift of intensive labor.

The Tableau is also the event where some of the best King Cake is served—my personal favorite. Tonight's King Cake looks about twelve feet long with purple, green and yellow sugar sprinkled onto the frosting that the pastry is cooked in, the shape and appearance resembling bread more than actual cake, and then somewhere inside is a small plastic baby. Tradition goes whoever gets the piece with the baby is responsible for buying the next King Cake—that or cook one like Angie can do.

"Claude," she says. "He's over there."

I see him. Mr. Val. He's actually dancing, though slow.

Breathing heavy, his mouth open and his bald head shining wet, Mr. Val takes five and returns to his table with a drink in hand while his wife goes to mingle.

"Okay, look. I'll call you later," I tell Angie.

She nods and goes to find her friends.

I approach the table.

"You know," I say to Mr. Val. "I don't think I ever congratulated you on making duke this year."

"You stupid son of a bitch," he says. "Are you out of your fucking mind? You think you're clever coming here? You think I won't make a scene? Well you ain't clever, you stupid son of a bitch. I'll cut your nuts off right here and now."

"Is that right?" I ask. I sit. "We were set up, Mr. Val. Anselmo raided the place maybe a second after we arrived."

"Well why don't we call him over here," he says. "Sort this out."

"Wait," I say. "If this was you. If you did this. Then— Sorry but I have to know. What did I do? Tell me what I did."

He sips his drink and crunches the ice in his mouth.

"Is it Angie? What, you don't want me with her so you decide to take me out? Fucking tell me what I did and you have my word. You'll never see me again."

"You damn right I'll never see you again. You'll be dead."

He stands and signals for Anselmo to come, and I go. I walk fast but not too fast, moving around and behind bodies on the dance floor.

Circling back from the other side of the auditorium, I watch Anselmo scan the floor.

He can't find me, and he leaves. Good. I follow the fucker to his car.

He starts it and I get in the backseat directly behind him. He looks in the rearview, and in that second, I pull his seatbelt around his throat. He chokes and I drive the barrel of my gun into the bottom of his neck.

"Settle down," I tell him. "Settle the fuck down. Good. Now listen to me, you fuck. It's real simple. I'm gonna ask you some questions, and you're gonna answer if you want to come out of this alive. Do we understand each other?" I pull tighter. "Do we understand each other?"

He chokes.

"How'd you know to come to Dupont's so early?" I ask. "Do you know who killed him?"

"Yeah. You," he says.

"No. Wrong answer. Tell me the version that people won't read about on the front page or I swear, they'll be reading about you in the obituaries."

"You might be brave," he says. "But you're not too smart and you won't be walking away from this alive. You hear me, Claude Verdell? Kill me. Kill me or I'll kill you the first chance I get."

"Promises. Promises," I say, recognizing this to be a waste of my time. I knock him out—it takes a few hits on his head—but he does go under, and I get out.

Unsure about my next move, I decide to sleep on it. I'm tired and still confused, still with no answers and no clear way of getting out of this mess.

Aboard my boat in the storage locker is a small radio that I turn on to fall asleep to.

When morning hits, and when the music stops for a breaking news alert, my eyes open.

Detective Evan Anselmo was found dead in his car last night, having been stabbed to death. My name is not mentioned, but the announcer states that investigators have a suspect in mind and will release more information in the near future.

"No. No fucking way."

I get to my feet and call Angie.

No words are spoken when she answers. All I hear are sobs.

"So I get you into the Tableau and you kill a cop? Is that what you are now, Claude? A cop killer?"

"Fucking for real? Listen to me. I didn't do this. Okay, Angie?

Sobs pour into my ear from the other end of the line. She's crying. Doesn't happen often.

"Angie, look. I—"

"No, Claude. Save it."

"You gotta believe me, Angie. I didn't do a damn thing but go and—I don't know what's happening. Okay? I wish to God I knew but I don't. Shit's fucked up and I've got no one."

"You know it really doesn't matter if you're telling the truth or not, Claude. This is the life you lead."

"I—I know. Look, I don't—I'm in trouble, and no matter what's happening, it all comes with the territory. I know that. But this could be the start of something else. Something better for us."

"What are you talking about?"

"I got a few bucks saved. Nothing that'll be too long-lasting but enough for now. Let's get out of here. Together. Come with me."

"Listen to you," she says. "My father would never stop chasing us."

"You're right. But after some time? After you go away for college in what, just a few months? Anything could happen. We can do anything we want, Angie. This is our life. Not his. So I go first and send for you. Why stay here? What's here for us?"

"How do you plan on getting out?" she asks.

"The parade," I tell her.

Cops will be looking for me at the bus stops. They'll be waiting for me at the airport and setting up roadblocks on all routes leaving Bayou Black.

But they won't be looking for me on a float. The parade travels from one side of town to the other before stopping at Murphy's parking lot where the floats are parked.

It's the biggest parking lot in all of Bayou Black, and adjacent to the bus station.

"Any way in hell you can get me on a float?" I ask Angie.

"My father's riding on the Duke's float this year, so there's room on his regular float," she says.

79

"What about beads?"

"It'll all be there for you," she says. "But you have to hurry. They finished the breakfast a little while ago and their getting ready. You gotta go right now."

It's Fat Tuesday—the final parade of the year until next season—and folks on the streets are going crazy. I bomb as many as I can with beads, in some cases not even opening the bags. I just throw entire bags of beads to the kids and watch them go wild. Their smiles, their joy and excitement—it's all contagious—and for the first time, I know what it's like to be alive. If this is in fact my final Mardi Gras, then it's only fitting I get to experience it from this side of the floats.

And for just a little while, I get to be someone else. I get to be somewhere else—the same place everyone else has gone, like the whole town is on a timeout from reality.

Hours seems like one—not even. The time passes and then it's all over.

We pull into Murphy's parking lot where families and friends of the riders on each float wait to great us, hoards of people everywhere and causing the perfect commotion I need to get away unseen.

I'll go to the bus station still in costume, of course, and not alone—it's the crowd, the riders and krewe I need to camouflage me more than anything—some will take a bus back to wherever they're going and I'll be among them.

There are so many people, but one stands out. Angie. She comes to greet our float and knows which one I am, even beneath the mask.

"I had to see you," she says. "I couldn't let you just leave. I came to say goodbye."

She hands me a piece of King Cake on a plastic plate.

"Far out. You made some?" I ask.

"For the entire float," she says, and I notice that most of them are already eating their pieces.

"No one's gotten the baby?" I ask, watching others who are pretty much finished with their pieces.

I take a bite, and then another. I can't help myself. Angie smiles, and then laughs when I try to force feed her a bite but I back off glad to save the rest of myself, and then I bite into something hard.

"Hey. I got it," I say, pulling the plastic baby from my mouth and holding it out in the palm of my hand. "How about that?"

Angie frowns.

"What? That's a good thing," I say. "Means I have to come back at some point. I have to buy the next King Cake."

"Oh, you won't be doing that," she says.

A rider from our float starts coughing, and he can't stop. He coughs until a violent choke takes hold of him. Another rider is about to approach him to help when he too falls sick, now on his knees coughing and gagging. It happens to all of them. The riders on our particular float, their faces are pale, and then blue.

"I needed them out of the way," Angie says to me. "I'll be able to retire the old man without much resistance now that they're out of the picture."

"What are you talking about, Angie?"

"I like to kill a lot of birds with one stone," she says. "Just like Dupont's."

"What? Dupont's? The jewelry store?" I ask.

"Mr. Dupont undermined my father at every turn. He shouldn't have been allowed to live, and my father let him. He's old now, Claude. He's slipping and it's time for new blood."

The raid on Dupont's put the murder on my crew, she explains, but more than that, it got rid of me permanently.

"What the—Why?" I ask.

"If anyone were ever to stand in the way of me taking over my father's empire, it was you," she says. "You're the only other one he would've passed it on to, and I can't allow that."

"But I—I loved you," I say.

"I loved you too," says Angie, the new queen of Bayou Black.

Ice cold with no expression on her face, she watches me keel over while crushing the baby in my fist—the one thing that held me to buying the next King Cake—a tradition that I'll be breaking, it seems.

But you know what they say.

81

Old traditions die hard.

Nathan Pettigrew was born and raised near New Orleans, Louisiana, and lives with his wife and pet rabbits in the Tampa area of Florida. His story "Dog Killer" was named among the Top 5 Winners and Finalists of the Writer's Digest *Eighth Annual Popular Fiction Awards for the crime category. Other stories appear in a number of exciting publications, including the award-winning pages of* Thuglit, *and* DarkMedia Original Fiction and Poetry, *which named his story "Roland The Conqueror" as one of their "most popular pieces of original horror to date" when it appeared in 2012. Visit Nathan at Solarcide.com or follow him on Twitter @NathanBorn2010.*

Official Author Page: http://solarcide.com/about/nathan-pettigrew/

WHO DAT? DAT THE INDIAN CHIEF!
BY
DEBRA H. GOLDSTEIN

Charlie Bones waited patiently. Not his usual style, but today was different. Today, he was an Indian Chief. An Indian Chief clad in a regal suit covered with hand- sewn sequins and feathers. He didn't know if he looked foolish or grand under the hundred-plus-pound weight of his costume, but he knew he was hot.

Standing in the doorway of what had been Al's Liquor Emporium, he decided that taking the chance of being recognized was better than sweating to death. With most of the businesses in New Orleans East destroyed by Katrina, he doubted anyone would pass him in the next few minutes.

He pulled his plumed headdress from his head revealing his full red 'fro. There was no hiding the contrast between his coal-colored skin and flaming hair. The combination had earned him plenty of nicknames at St. Aug before he'd learned to use his fists to demand respect. Now nobody dared call him Redtop, Bonehead, or any of those long ago schoolboy names to his face.

Charlie knew he needed to get his headdress back on, but it felt good without his masked head covering. He gently wiped the sweat from his brow with one of his feather-covered sleeves before stepping from the doorway to peer down the street. A block ahead of him, he could see the top of the gang's flag. From the erect position of the huge staff decorated with feathers and his group's symbol, he could tell that Spyboy, two blocks ahead of Flagboy, had yet to relay the sighting of another gang.

Try as he might to be politically correct, he had trouble referring to the other street groups as Krewes. The more typical New Orleans Mardi Gras parades had been lily white, named after Roman or Greek Gods, and used a royalty structure that included kings, queens and pages. Slavery and racism had kept his people from being part of those Mardi Gras Krewes, so they created their own. They paid their respect to the native New Orleans Indians who helped them escape the tyranny of slavery by making up Indian tribe Krewe names that incorporated their street or ward gang names.

Their parades had no set routes. Until recently, they had been a time to settle scores because the New Orleans police were too busy with traditional Mardi Gras activities to interfere. Today's more civilized tribal Krewes used dance and ritual chants to celebrate the distinctive style and art of their respective costumes. Making sure he tucked the knife between his waist feathers so it could be easily retrieved, he feared history might be repeated.

The waiting was getting to him. He felt like he was on a stakeout, except this time Charlie was unsure of where his quarry was. A quick movement of Flagboy's staff caught his eye. He watched the circles and angles Flagboy made in the air telling him that Spyboy had spotted the tribe Charlie had instructed him to locate.

Charlie glanced down at his costume. The sequins he had sewn on his vest sparkled in the sun, but there was no question that the jeweled eye of the eagle sitting over his heart was what brought his costume to life. His fingers lingered on it for just a moment before he put his headdress on and grabbed the thick stick he had leaned against the wall of the doorway.

Jumping into the center of the road, he let out three loud whoops and then deliberately raised his rod and banged it sharply on the asphalt in front of the Emporium. He walked about five feet forward and wailed in a birdlike falsetto. Ahead of him, Flagboy mimicked his bird sound and struck the ground hard with his staff. The two of them ran through the same scenario three more times.

From his vantage point, Charlie saw the few uncostumed second-liners, who had been singing or playing their tambourines for any onlookers standing between Flagboy and him, stop their entertaining to listen to their exchange. As Charlie and the second liners walked forward, following the angle of Flagboy's now moving staff, the liners whispered his staccato refrain.

Charlie heard the other Krewe before he saw it. He smiled at the sounds of laughter and cries only children can make. Tradition dictated that children didn't march in the Indian Parades because of the violence associated with them, but Father Tom had laid the mothers' fears of their children wanting to join the Indians to rest. His tribe ranged from altar boys to youthful scoundrels, and they followed him as if he were the Pied Piper.

Most of his congregants and students thought of him in that way until Katrina, but the hurricane changed the course of Father Tom's youth ministry. Flood damage to the building's structure, the number of evacuated parishioners who never returned, and the loss of businesses in the area made his church one that the diocese deemed unsalvageable. Like many others, it became part of a consolidated parish. Father Tom still was searching for his position in the new order, but as Charlie had hoped, he probably hadn't lost his place leading his juvenile Krewe.

As the two tribes neared the same point, the old and young of the Krewes mingled together dancing and singing in the street, but they parted to give the two Chiefs room to approach each other. Once the distance between them narrowed to a few yards, the second liners closed in around them.

The two chiefs circled each other, carefully keeping the distance of their huge sticks between them. For a moment, Charlie stared at the opposing Chief's costume of green and gold feathers. He tried to find an unmasked area to determine if the Chief was truly Father Tom, but there was no exposed area of skin.

The edges of a full-faced satin mask that pointed out like a beak were tucked under the ridge of his headdress. Soft tufted feathers sweeping out behind him further accentuated the image of a bird taking flight. Different patches of sequins and feathers incorporated into his costume portrayed stories important to the Chief or his people. They included an image of an eagle similar to the one that adorned Charlie's chest, but its sequined eye lacked the radiance of Charlie's jewel.

As the two faced off, Charlie yelled as loudly as he could. "Humba!"

The other Chief didn't respond to Charlie's demand that he bow and pay him respect. Instead, he stepped into Charlie's private space and began to sway and chant. With each beat of his foot, the volume of his voice rose until he was screaming. "Me no humba. *You* humba."

The two moved toward each other playing out the motions of their war dance. When they were close enough so that they could not be overheard, Charlie said: "Looking good, baby. Looking good!"

His nemesis nodded his head in acknowledgement of the compliment, but didn't return it. "Jewels, Charlie? You gone uptown on me, man?"

"Maybe," Charlie said. He'd forgotten only uptown Indians used jewels to finish off their costumes. He figured in the end Father Tom wouldn't hold it against him.

The second Chief stretched his head back and raised his stick acknowledging the sky and sun. He whooped and hollered, ignoring Charlie. In that moment, Charlie whacked his stick against the man's head and neck. Surprised, he whipped his neck back down so quickly that his mask slipped free from his headdress, allowing Charlie to catch a glimpse of his alabaster skin.

"What's with you?"

"Just making sure it was you," Charlie said.

"As if you didn't know?"

Charlie extended his hand with the stick toward his albino friend, but Father Tom backed away. "After all these years, you didn't know it was me? What's got into you Charlie? Losing your police detective skills?"

Charlie didn't move as Father Tom made a show of examining his costume from afar. He let Father Tom set the pace for their dance, much as he had let him lead when their differences had brought them together as kids. Back then, who would have thought the two school misfits would grow up to tend the community's soul? Father Tom finally stopped in front of Detective Charlie Bones and bammed his stick two times.

"Humba."

For the crowd's benefit, Charlie shook his head and put his hand over his eagle's eye while loudly proclaiming "No humba." He moved closer to Father Tom and let his stickless hand slide to his waist. "Forgive me father, for I have sinned," he whispered, pulling his knife from its sheath.

He raised the knife between their chests, keeping his focus on his friend's colorless eyes. As Charlie made a swift cut, he felt Father Tom's hand close around his wrist to wrestle the knife from him. "No," he said, as the knife dropped from his fingers, landing next to his now forgotten stick. "You've got it wrong! I'm seeking redemption," Falling to his knees, Charlie pulled at his chest with one hand while instinctively reaching out for his knife with the other before Father Tom could cover it with his foot.

"I humba," he shouted, ducking a blow from Father Tom's stick while shoving his knife back into its hiding place. The stick glanced off his left shoulder. "I humba!"

Father Tom permitted Charlie to pick up his rod and stand upright from his cowered position on the ground, but he held his stick in readiness. The two squared off again, but this time, Charlie bowed to his opposition and with a beat of his retrieved staff and gestures from his arms acknowledged the majesty of Father Tom's costume.

The children surrounding them cheered Charlie's submission while the crowd applauded their Chiefs' throwback portrayal of the historical violence of the Indian parades. Thinking the tribal display was finished, the two spyboys and flagboys resumed their assigned tasks while most of the onlookers and Krewe members fell in together to march and dance in a relaxed parade formation as they searched for more tribes to confront.

With a flourish that appeared to still be part of their dance, Charlie took his hand from his chest and extended it to Father Tom. "Take this. It's for the collection box."

Father Tom shifted his stick to steady it against the ground, but kept his free hand lying at his side.

Charlie turned his hand palm upward so Father Tom could see the diamond lying in his bloodstained palm.

"You're bleeding."

"Must have nicked myself when I cut off the eagle's eye. Guess I shouldn't have been quite so dramatic in the way I transported it to you." He leaned forward to press the stone into Father Tom's hand.

"Where did you get this?"

Charlie ignored the question. "Don't worry about that."

Father Tom stared at the stone. "I don't understand, but I'm pretty sure it isn't something I can accept."

"Tom, look around you." Charlie waved his hand around the desolate street they stood on and then reached out and pulled Father Tom's arm to make him turn to the vacant lot behind him. "Wasn't that where your church was?"

Father Tom nodded, but Charlie didn't stop. He pointed further up the street. "Think about the houses, stores and people who lived and worked in our neighborhood before Katrina. Most all of them are gone. Tell me, what's left for those still here?"

"Hope."

"Hope doesn't buy school uniforms, medical treatment or put food into bellies."

"And crime does?"

"Sometimes, but don't worry," Charlie assured Father Tom. "This isn't one of those times. I wasn't a blue looter. That diamond was part of my planned masking before Katrina ever came along. I wanted to use the jewel on our eagle patch to show people how far we've soared."

"So, why give it to me now?" Father Tom asked, closing his hand around the diamond.

"Because I think your team can do a lot more good with that gem than I can, although," he said, puffing out his chest,

88

"I've got to tell you it was a pleasure strutting from my house with it on my patch this morning."

"I'm missing something here."

"Tom, I've never been a saint, but I took an oath to enforce the law. You of all people know how horrible the looting, trespassing, and disregard for human dignity was with Katrina. Bad enough when it was some punk, but I couldn't stand by without saying something when a few of the blue went bad. Today's parade isn't over for this Indian yet, but just in case, maybe after everything I've seen and done this past year, that diamond can buy me some forgiveness and redemption?"

Father Tom didn't answer. He slipped the diamond into his pocket and banged his stick to let his tribe know he was moving on. He took a few steps away from Charlie, but then turned back and made an elaborate bow toward him. "Who Dat? Dat *the* Indian Chief."

Judge Debra H. Goldstein's debut novel, Maze in Blue, *a mystery set on the University of Michigan's campus in the 1970's, received a 2012 IPPY Award. She also is the author of several short stories and non-fiction essays including* A Political Cornucopia, Legal Magic, Grandma's Garden *and* Maybe I Should Hug You. *Judge Goldstein lives in Birmingham, Alabama with her husband whose blood runs Crimson.*

Website: www.DebraHGoldstein.com
Blog: "It's Not Always A Mystery"
http://DebraHGoldstein.wordpress.com
She also blogs for The Stiletto Gang:
http://thestilettogang.blogspot.com/

WHY THE MASK
BY
PAUL WARTENBERG

"Why the mask?"

She asked this, slipping the ceramic smooth visage into place. It fit, cool and curved, to her face.

The mask-maker did not turn to look at her. "Because you won't be able to approach him any other way."

She turned to face the glass window that dominated one side of the room. With the darkness outside and the candlelight indoors, it worked as a mirror, bends and warps distorting the reflection. "It's only the mask I can take with me, then?"

Another man's voice came from another room, the open doorway leading into the dark. "It's best that way. You know what he's like. He has guards by now. They'll be checking everyone who approaches."

She kept the mask on as she walked to the doorway, staring into that darkness. "What if they take the mask?"

Laughter, more of a chuckle than anything, from both of the men. The mask-maker in the lit room turned in his chair, taking his eye off the mask he was painting. "More custom than anything else, miss. Be rude to take the mask off you this time of year, with the festival. Rules. Doubt the boss-man would mind the mask, anyway."

The mask-maker nodded at what she was wearing. "Did you need me to add any more color to your face there, miss?"

She felt the mask, wondering if she should slide it off and re-examine the makeup applied to the surface. She didn't take the time to examine the artwork that close. "I'm sure it's fine."

"Of course it's fine." The voice from the dark room was closer. The man stepped into the light, tall and strong. He placed a hand on her shoulder. "This is the best man in the Thirteenth ward with shaping the clay into art."

"Praise will only go so far," the mask-maker answered with a grin. "I didn't do my best work on this, you asked for discretion so you're getting it. It's different from what I usually work with; it was good you brought most of what you needed to make it. I even used new brushes and strokes so no one could identify my hand on it. Still, that mask will serve you well."

Her friend nodded to the artist with a solemn look. "Is there anything else you need?"

The mask-maker shook his head. "Everything's prepared for you upstairs." He started to say a name, then stopped. "Forgot, you're insisting on no names. My friends should have everything else you asked for taken of. You can check."

She nodded, fingering the edges of the mask. The mask-maker had already seen her face, but that didn't seem to be the issue. Part of her wanted to feel more comfortable wearing it. "I do thank you, sir. For the work you've done. I hope all things go well, when they happen."

The mask-maker chuckled, showing something of a smile of white teeth, made glaring by a gap of side teeth knocked out of his mouth. "Sir, she called me 'sir'. This girl's too polite for her own good."

"It's who she is," the tall man answered, and he nodded to her when she looked at him. "It's a busy day tomorrow, let's get you to sleep."

The building was dim-lit in the hallways and stairwells, the walls thin to where she could hear conversations both pleasant and raging as she was led upstairs. The small apartment that had been set aside for them was brighter lit, there was that.

"No expense spared," the tall man noted with a smile as he closed the door behind them, glancing about the small kitchen set at the entrance.

"Not a matter to be bothered," she answered. "This isn't a bad place to be tonight."

He kept smiling and walked into the small seating area where boxes and wrapped items piled up atop a plain-cloth sofa. "Did you want to check everything they've got for us?"

"It's late." She followed him, then walked past for a doorway leading to a small bedroom. "It can wait for morning."

"We'll need to leave before anyone will notice." He placed his hands on both her shoulders, brushing aside her shoulder length auburn hair before rubbing down along her arms.

She sighed, leaning back against his chest. "At this point, I don't care for anyone to know."

"I do." He let go, walking past her into the room, reaching for a lamp. The extra light didn't brighten the room somehow, it cast more shadows with him standing there.

"Which is why you've never told me your name." The mask on her face hid her sad expression.

"I have." The man half-turned from her, unbuttoning the vest he wore and then the shirt underneath it.

She raised a hand, wiggling her fingers as she counted. "You've given me six different names, haven't you? I'd lost count."

The vest was draped over a dresser, the shirt unbuttoned but left parted to expose the man's coffee-toned skin. Muscular but slim. He faced her now, half-sliding the shirt off his shoulders. "I've given you seven names, actually. One of them is the name my mother gave me."

"But not a name you're known by, I'd wager." She leaned against the doorway, watching him undress. "I'll be guessing all my life which one is it if you never tell me."

He turned, doing what he could to keep the shadows covering his back, but she could see the edge of the scarring along his side. He kept smiling as he stripped down to his shorts, but didn't answer her.

"Lightning Joe then," she sighed. "I should call you Lightning Joe."

He laughed at that. "You're going with the name I used in Kansas City?"

"Are you telling me that's not a real name?"

He bit his tongue, glanced toward the bed, kept smiling. "Not going to answer that. I want to keep you guessing."

"You always will."

Lightning Joe rolled onto the bed. It seemed sturdy but narrow, barely enough room for even one to rest there. "I want you to keep that mask on tonight."

She slid the mask off her face. "Not tonight. I want you to see me smile before we sleep," she grinned.

Morning was sunless, cloudy, with a fresh chill to the breeze.

She dressed the way a woman would if she were out shopping, not with extravagance but with an air of money to her. Fancy yet sensible, with her purse slung over one arm and some of the bags containing her excursion supplies dangling over the other. If anyone noticed her, they'd not be concerned about what she carried. They would notice the veil draped over her face, white lace with flower patterns. It would be fashionable to wear one, depending on the time and place. But it hid her face in the daylight, and people would stare as they tended to do, looking up from the newspapers describing the threats of war in Europe and Asia, wanting to see what might hide underneath the patterns.

Lightning Joe had dressed for work, pushing a handcart with the boxes piled on. He kept a few paces behind her, providing some distance in case anyone paid attention. He'd been in the city enough times for enough people to know him. No one here knew her.

They were separated when the trolley had room enough for her but not for him. She tried to exchange a glance with him, but he shook his head without looking her way. She reached the French Quarter alone, as the breakfast tables were cleared away for the coming lunch, surrounded by festive party-goers who always seem to have started the Mardi Gras and never end it.

She entered the courtyard of the house she was renting. The owners were infamously pious Catholics who took leave each year to avoid the debauchery. Lightning Joe made arrangements this year through some of the friends he'd made over his visits here, convincing the aged married couple they

94

needed a house-sitter to ensure no one would wreck or rob while they were away in Europe – France this year, as Fascist Italy seemed so gauche to visit – on pilgrimage. And by convincing it meant having his friends rob one or three of the neighbors along the street, discreetly of course, while his more upstanding allies among the local police force dropped none-too-subtle hints. Getting them to rent to a "visiting lady scholar" who happened to have cash on hand to help fund a more enlightened overseas trip was even easier.

She waited a half-hour before Lightning Joe arrived at the gate. "You shouldn't be so nervous," he told her once they were indoors.

"Anything could go wrong while we're apart," she answered, hugging him for a minute before he insisted they continue working.

The work they did involved setup, putting parts together, fixing clothing and items, retouching the mask as needed. She admired the mask in the daytime, a beautifully smooth creation with a series of kissing marks painted into the surface, everywhere but the ceramic lips themselves remaining untouched and pale. The only thing she changed on the mask was the small red dot on the spot between the eyes and just above the nose ridge, rubbing it away to hide what it meant. She remembered the explanation and that dot was no longer needed.

They almost stopped for lunch, except that it began to rain. "Oh no," she said, stepping through a glass-paned door into a back courtyard. She walked into the middle of the garden planted there, surrounded by green palm leaves bouncing as the heavy drops landed. "This can't happen, not now not like this..."

Lightning Joe followed her out into the garden, looking up into the sky past the three-story walls enclosing the small alcove, letting the rain fall into his face, eyes half-closed and squinting from the water hitting him. He smiled, teeth bared in a delirious joyful way. "This is just a light storm, that's all. It'll come and go. They won't cancel the parade for this, none of the celebrations." He lowered his face, droplets rolling down his cheeks. "Relax."

She reached up to kiss him. Wrapped one arm over his shoulder, drawing him down toward her, while the other arm slid around his waist to steady herself against him. It didn't work; she pulled too hard and they fell into the garden, crushing some flowers.

They laughed and kissed as the rain fell, with her pulling at Lightning Joe's shirt to unbutton it again, trying to take off the cold soaking thing to get at the warm skin underneath. "No, no, not now," he whispered, kissing her and then lifting himself up, pulling away.

He led her back inside, to the bedroom, to where fresh clothes awaited them. "Afternoon, will be night before you know it," he told her, passing her a towel as he grabbed one for himself. "I'll need to go soon, to get some of this gear in place where you'll need it."

"Does it have to be this soon?" She asked, holding only that towel between them.

He smiled at her, but shook his head. "Tonight. Save everything for tonight."

The light of the streets dominated the sunless twilight sky. By this time on the clocks, by her reckoning of day, there should have been a sunset marking the divide into night.

She may have been the only one paying attention to the sky, even as the cloud cover threatened more rain to come. Everyone else walking the streets outside the house gate were too attentive to the beer bottles in their hands, or the lovers wrapped within each other arms. An ongoing parade of revelers, all of them masked, all of them celebrating, all of them unprepared for her.

She checked herself one last time. Combing the flame-red hair back off her shoulders, down to the point below the small of her back. Making sure the mask she wore was secure at the edge of her hairline, the surface polished and painted. Tapping the short-heeled boots against the pavement, timing herself to a song beat playing in her mind.

Satisfied, she hummed the song now, loud enough to vibrate the mask against her cheeks. Feeling it was now time, she opened the gate to step out into the orange-lit street. Stepped out into the New Orleans night with her mask on.

Only her mask.

And the boots. She considered going barefoot, but previous walks down Bourbon Street had convinced her that avoiding broken bottle shards was next to impossible.

There was a surge, a thrill, not the chilled air that follows a spring downpour, that worked its way along her spine as she walked into Mardi Gras. Whatever modesty she had facing the world, even with her veil hiding what had been done, even with the mask she wore all these years, none of that mattered in the moment. Her exposed porcelain skin meant nothing, not even the risk of arrest or worse. It was something about what she was doing this night, how she was going to present herself to make her path easier, that somehow going naked meant the most sense to her. This was easier.

No one even seemed to notice for the first three blocks. It wasn't until she reached a bar front on the corner of Bourbon Street that a drunken reveler shouted his surprise. Everyone – men and women – turned to watch as she passed. What surprised her was the lack of wolf-calls, the seeming respectful distance the crowd suddenly presented her. The audacity, perhaps, of taking Mardi Gras to an extreme few people had dared before. Either that or it happened too often, she couldn't be sure of which.

She heard the footsteps begin behind her as she reached Bourbon and turned east, into the growing crowd, along the parade route that would be used for tonight's festivities. Through the eye holes of the ceramic mask, she noticed as wave upon wave of watchers turned their attention to her. The entire city seemed to see her as she walked, exposed and hidden all at once. The voices would turn from drunken shouting to slurred murmurs, some approving, some awed, some envious and questioning.

If there was anything of the moment, none of the men seemed to want to grab her, claim her in some manly fashion. It may have seemed rude to them, perhaps fearful that this was a temptation, or dreaded risking interrupting some ritual or theatrical performance. She thought of legend, of a story about a

97

naked lady honored in protest, and wondered if that legend protected her now.

There was only one patrolman on her path as she walked Bourbon Street. The crowd hushed as she approached, and he turned to see just what the lack of commotion was all about.

He was graying, fatherly, but with a hard face that didn't smile or show sympathy. He stood in her path. She stopped, knowing this could be the end of her attempt, but refusing to run or hide. She had nowhere to go now, having gone this far.

The patrolman gave her the once-over. He seemed to glare into her mask, looking for the color of her eyes perhaps. His stone face scowled just a bit more after a minute of considering her and this bacchanal overreach. "Ma'am, just to let you know we got a law against this sort of thing."

And then he stepped aside.

There was a grand cheer from the surrounding audience, and she bowed gracefully toward the patrolman as she continued her march towards the warehouses. It was still a long walk, but she kept going. The crowds didn't. They followed for a block or two, then turned back to where they wanted to be, to where the parties were still happening, content enough to have witnessed her nudity as a work of art. Convinced she was part of tonight's parade, all part of the show for their amusement after all.

Some of the parade floats were already deployed outside of the warehouses, waiting for passengers and final touches of banners and wreaths. Some horse-drawn had their stallions in place, impatiently lifting their legs as they waited. The horses watched her as she walked past, curious but nothing more.

"You there!"

She stopped. This was the true moment. She turned her head but not her stance. Two men approached, one dressed in fancy garb of the mummery, the older gent in the pressed button suit of a businessman. She noticed the bulk in the button-suit's armpit, grateful that the gun making that bump was safely put away.

The button-suit guard gave her the once-over, much like the patrolman did. His scowl was more menacing. "What the hell are you doing here?"

She steeled her resolve, doing her best not to quiver as she spoke. "I was called."

"Who the hell called you?"

She shook her head, letting the long hair brush against her backside. "He didn't say. I was called to appear before the King."

The button-suit waved a hand at her. "Arms up. Up!"

She complied. She took a step further to place her hands behind her head, interlocking her fingers. It forced herself to stand more upright, more outward, which had the desired effect on the costumed guard who involuntarily cackled.

The button-suit back-handed his partner. "You're asking for a bleeding if you don't settle." He kept his eyes on her. "What the hell are you here for, trying to cause a distraction or something?"

"I was called." She stuck to her story. "There was a request for a girl. Present myself to the King of the Fool's Festival. Told me to come like this. Present myself, as a proper offering."

The costumed guard grinned at his partner. "It sounds like something Henry would call in for an early supper."

"Shut it." Button-suit kept glowering at the naked masked woman. "We weren't told. Nobody I know would put in the call."

"Please ask them, one of them had to." she replied. "Ask the King if an offering was needed tonight. Otherwise I came here for nothing."

The older guard grimaced. "Search her," he growled.

The costumed guard grinned ever wider. "Oh, this will be a..."

"Never mind that!" Button-suit pushed him back, realizing his mistake. He stepped closer to her, reaching with his hands into her hair, feeling the strands, rubbing the edges of the mask but refusing to take it off her. He glared into her eyes as he leaned in. "Those boots. Take them off."

It took little effort, and she handed each boot to the button-suit guard. He felt each one for something hidden, a razor perhaps, then decided to drop them to the ground. "Leave them here. Walk."

He pushed the costumed guard to step ahead of him, and then gestured to her to follow. She nodded and kept pace behind the bulky reveler. A group of other men, most of them dressed for the festival, watched them approach and each of them made an inappropriate comment or wolf-whistle.

"You lot! Enough!" The tone from the button-suit guard was enough to settle them down. "Where the hell is Henry tonight?"

"Out on business," was a reply from one of the costumed men. "Making arrangements with Juan regarding..." There was a pause. "Regarding, you know, stuff, from that other place with stuff."

"The peppers and spices kind of stuff," another voice giggled nearby, and half the krewe joined in with the laugh.

"Shut! Up!" Button-suit waved a thumb back at her. "This bitch is claiming she was called to service our boy tonight. Anyone know a thing about it? Did Henry put in a call?"

A long moment of confusion. Murmurs and questions among them. This was where the bluff had to pan out, she knew. The biggest gamble, but the easiest lie to pull off, because none of these men would want to admit they didn't know otherwise, to turn away a naked willing woman from the likes of their hedonist boss.

"I know, I think," another voice, different from the first two, came from the group, "that Henry made a request like usual. Just not sure about the delivery, you know, when the time would be? Not the first time a woman's been brought out here either, has it? Just not sure about the packaging though, usually they get shipped wrapped." There was a wave of laughter. "Not that anyone should complain, the package looks nice as is..."

"Fine, fine," Button-suit answered. He turned to face her. "Say nothing. Stay behind me. You do anything stupid, you'll hurt." He leaned in to whisper. "The kind of pain that takes days to apply and a lifetime to wash away, ya follow?"

"I understand," she whispered back in complete sincerity.

It was a brief stride to the warehouse doorway where another business-suited man stood alert. He admired the approaching naked woman, same as the others, but said nothing, giving a nod to the Button-suit guard in acknowledgment. The door unlocked, and she was guided inside.

The warehouse's interior was stacked with boxes, wooden and scented, surrounding an open spot in the middle of the floor where a large float had been constructed and decorated. Much like for any Mardi Gras, it was garish and colorful, except this was even more opulent. Real gold plates mounted into the awnings, rather than brass or copper. Proper sails rather than bedsheets. A small pirate boat designed to sail the streets of 1938 New Orleans.

On the top desk of this boat sat a man upon a purple plush throne. The seat was larger than any common man could fit into it. He fit well, not obese but bulky, firm and stout with a hardened barrel of a chest. The outfit he wore – half-jester, half-king – did not seem to match the style of the float. It was as though they had a mind for one style and then changed it for another without concern.

The meal the fool ate was appropriate for a king. A large plate of blackened chicken, bread rolls strewn over plate and table, a massive bottle of whiskey sitting next to a smaller yet impressive unopened bottle of rum. He seemed intent on pulling more meat off the bones as the two guards escorted her up the ship's boarding plank onto the lower deck. "Captain?" Button-suit asked, getting within range.

There was a grumble and a mixture of slurred words before a coherent phrase was answered back. "Approach, get closer what now. What is this?"

Button-suit took the steps upward to the top deck, blocking the naked woman from his Captain's view. "Got a girl here, says she was called to you. Know anything about that?"

A burp. More grumbling, before the fool-king answered back. "Of course, of course, know everything, don't I? Ought to know. Let's take a look eh? Look at her, see if she's worth the money..."

Button-suit finished his walk onto the top deck, giving her a chance to step up and present herself. She pliantly placed both arms behind her long hair, presenting her charms as best as possible. It had the right effect. "Ohhh yes, yes she will do nicely

101

tonight on my lap, make the lot stare the whole parade down won't it ahah!" The seated fool-king gestured to her to step closer. Once she reached the table he waved a hand at the dining table between them. "Wouldn't be polite, ur, impolite, not to offer this galley wench a taste of the delights aboard this boat?"

"I am fine tonight, King of the Festival," she answered with a courteous tone. She took a moment to glance about the warehouse, pretending to view the float. "This is a fine ship you captain tonight, sir."

The fool-king laughed, grabbing the whiskey bottle and taking a drink. "Ought to be, heh, borrowing it from another krewe, they did a good job of it, after all. Well then, let's get to it." He gestured her to approach him, then turned in his throne to glare at Button-suit. "And you, wanna stay and watch perhaps! Get back to work, like I pay you! Parade starts any minute now!"

She didn't turn to watch, keeping her focus on her target, but heard the footsteps of the two guards stumbling against the wood desk. She smiled under the mask, wondering if her real smile matched the mask's smile.

"There now. Heh. Have a sheet m'dear," the fool-king slurred, "have a seat."

There was only one place to sit. She lifted one leg to straddle his thigh, and slid the other to put herself completely in his lap. She looked closely at his face. The years had added a few wrinkles to the brow, and to the corners of his eyes, but the stubble of his cheeks and chin remained darkish red, and those eyes the dull brown as before.

She rubbed his chest, leaning in close with her face-mask, but offering nothing for him to kiss, even as he licked his lips, and not for cleaning away the food he'd just eaten. She slid her hands up along the sides of the throne, feeling the edge of the wooden seat, reaching up over his head to check the hardness of the chair's cresting point. It gave him a better view of her body, she knew, and she felt it as he leaned in to nuzzle, but she took the moment not to mind. "This is a strong throne you sit on, my King," she whispered.

He only laughed in reply, coughing a bit and then lifting up the bottle to drink more whiskey.

"Shall we do it here, then, upon your throne?" she asked as innocently as possible.

The fool-king laughed hard, letting the bottle slip from his hands as he gripped her hips, pulling her downward. "Ah, yes! Yes! But we need to remove the king's clothes, don't we? How hard can that be from where you're perched on my lap, little birdie?"

"It's easy, I would think," she replied. "It's as easy as me taking off my mask."

She slid it downward, slowly, careful not to disturb the hair. The frozen smile of the mask gave way to the nervous twitch of her real one. She let him see her face. The body she knew he'd never recognize, it had been years and she had grown since that distant night. But the face, her face...

He noticed the scar near her eye right away. He burped and flinched at the same time. "I can see why you wore the mask on the way over here, birdie. Didn't you think to wear some make-up to it, pretty yourself up?"

She smiled, and not a warm or laughing one. "I didn't want to hide it away under powder or paint, if that's what you meant. And after all, I wanted you to get a chance to recognize your own work."

She didn't stop to see how his reaction would be to what she said. She swung the mask above her head, both hands to the sides of it, and swung down with just enough force upon the ridge of the throne. Catching the blow upon that one spot between the eyes of the mask.

It shattered, leaving behind two large shards as she'd wanted it to be. One in each hand, a jagged point like daggers to each shard. Only a great mask-maker could craft such precise weapons.

She glanced down as she swung both arms inward, aiming. The fool-king still hadn't reacted to what she'd said, either the whiskey or confusion slowing his response. One hand still clasped to her hip, the other dangling off the throne's armrest not even reaching for the lost bottle.

The mask itself was designed to be soft but the surviving shards were meant to remain hard, solid as steel, sharp for cutting. Into the neck, exposed as the fool-king had left himself looking upward to her body, to her iron-cold gaze as she shoved and shoved harder.

She aimed for the arteries, for the tongue behind that devil's drunken smile, shoving hard enough to reach the brain if she could. Neither shard broke as they dug into flesh and muscle, avoiding bone, shedding blood along the cutlines without spurting or gushing.

It took a second before the fool-king even realized there was pain, that this was an attack. Larger, stronger than she was, the hand against her hip clenched, trying to dig into her before shoving her lightweight form off his lap. She tumbled, but the one-handed shoved pushed her sideways, not back onto the table, and she tumbled free onto the wooden deck.

He tried to stand up, to scream, to gasp. He lifted his hips up, pushing his back off the throne, but something caught him. His robe tugged against the armrest and he collapsed back into the purple cushions. Whatever noises he tried to make through his opening mouth, it only came out as wheezing groans. He clenched his throat with his free hand, clawing at it, trying to dig out the shard caught over his windpipe and voicebox. The groaning turned into gurgling. There wasn't as much blood spilling onto his neck as she had imagined. Perhaps the blood was falling down a different path, into his lungs...

She didn't want to stay and watch, despite the necessity of making certain her revenge had become reality. The Fool-King was dead, despite the flailing trapped body. It was only a matter of time now.

She hurried down the boat ramp into the warehouse, glancing about for what she needed. The doors were guarded. The windows were in sight. Except in one place, the windows between warehouses.

She reached the second floor office, where a bright light shone directly into the room from the warehouse across the way. The window was panel, and opened like a door onto a fire escape. But the fire escape wasn't what she needed. It was the rope dangling in front of her.

104

She grinned like a little girl of twelve again, yanking on the rope as a series of pulleys dragged a thin gurney across from the nearby warehouse. The warehouse of Juliano the Fool-King of the Mississippi River was well-guarded this Mardi Gras, but the surrounding ones were not. Especially the one where Lightning Joe and his business partners had provided some work to help getting the floats prepared.

She hopped into the gurney, taking time to lean back and close the window behind her. The guards were bound to check every escape route, and this window was the most likely place, but she wanted to make it hard for them to see how she did it. Once secured, she pulled a different direction on the rope, swinging the machinery back over to the neighboring warehouse, keeping an eye downward to make sure no patrolling guard thought to look up...

She stepped as quietly as possible off the gurney, then took the minute she needed to break apart as much of the gear as she could. The burlap material she wrapped around herself, finally warming her body after this hour of nakedness. The rope she tied under one shoulder, two of the pulleys she took apart, hiding the mechanics as best she could. The remaining bits looked like a normal part of the warehouse.

This warehouse was slightly more active once she exited the empty office on this side of her escape path. Another float, this one also horse-drawn, was getting its final touch-ups of banners and flowers. A handful of krewe members stood along the flatbed, wrapping things into place, but none of them seemed to pay attention to the shadowy figure sneaking through the half-empty cartons lining the far wall. The side door at the other end of the warehouse swung open and then closed with no one the wiser.

She walked, barefoot, as best she could, knowing not to slide off the burlap hiding the body she just recently exposed. The hair was loose upon her head now, however, and she needed to find the next spot on the path where Lightning Joe said he had what she'd need to clean off the evidence.

The barrel trashcan with flame was next along the path, walking the alley away from the warehouses and away from

Bourbon Street, but there were already some men, bagged-dressed worse than she was at the moment, warming their hands to the fire. They noticed her and her long hair and some whistled at her, but she kept walking. This step wasn't available to her now.

Instead something else made itself available. A sudden burst of rainfall caught her in the middle of the street, along with a handful of other party-goers en route to the festivities just blocks away. Many of them ran, laughing or crying in disappointment, but she stood there, in the middle of the street, letting it fall. It was just as the afternoon rainfall had been, cold and dripping but not hard, not drowning. It washed her body as she opened up the burlap covering, washing away anything that might be blood or foodstain, and just as she leaned her head back into the water, it knocked the red wig off her head, exposing the short auburn hair. The wig washed into the street, caught into a drainage path, rolling into the sewers just as easily as if it'd been thrown away.

She kept moving at that point, hoping no one had seen her in the half-dark street, knowing she wasn't clear yet of any suspicion or pursuers.

The next spot was set aside in an abandoned store front, but one with the lights left on. She tried the door, unlocked, and entered. She turned off the light and went to work, pulling the storefront dummies away from the window and into the shadow.

This was the other reason why she decided to make her approach to Juliano's warehouse in the nude. She brought as little as she could that needed to be thrown away. The boots were already gone. The mask, used. The long wig was the only other thing she worried, and the rainfall took care of that better than a barrel fire. All she had to do now was take the replacement clothes left for her here, and not leave anything else.

The rope was left to dangle over a hook in the back of the empty store. The wet burlap she still needed with the rain outside. But from here she had her sandals, the knee-length black skirt, the tight pullover harlequin top, and the red veil that draped only over half her face, the side with her scar. It took her two minutes, and she left by locking the door behind her.

The rain had let up some, but she kept the burlap over her as a blanket to shield her, hurrying down the half-lit street that grew brighter the closer she reached the parade route. Two blocks away, she came to one last spot, finding two large hand-woven fake feathers. The crates they rested upon looked like a proper spot to drape a wet burlap cover, and she exchanged the items.

Waving the feathers above her head, as though dancing her way into the crowds, she moved as openly as possible to the world. She passed many of the street crowds that greeted her nude form earlier, including the patrolman, now teamed with a handful of other officers making their presence known among the festive mob. She danced her way up the street, flinging her feathers where she could, encircling the occasional drunkard who wanted to get closer before twirling away with a laugh. Everyone was having fun in the moment, herself included.

She left the feathers outside a music hall, planting them into a potted palm at the doorway to the amusement of the door-greeters, and wandered her way through the packed crowds to a reserved table where she sat alone. The crowd was a mix of colors, both costumes and skin, although the dividing lines for that were left pretty clear as the whites sat closer to the jazz band performing for the night.

She sat far enough back to where the colored audience was within an arm's reach of her. Or least a lean-over from one table to the next. She felt him sitting there, behind her now, although she didn't see him earlier when she came in. She leaned back so she could hear him, knowing he had to speak to her.

Lightning Joe's voice was soft enough to stay hidden underneath the music ringing through the hall into the street outside the open windows. "I heard of what you did."

"I hope you're not angry," she whispered back.

"Just surprised. But it was clever. Everyone's going to be looking for a naked girl now."

She glanced at the doorway. There was no sign of commotion by the door-greeters making sure only the invited were let in. No sign yet that the body of the Fool-King had even been discovered. Depended on when the parade began, most likely. She imagined the parade continuing on with that body of the Fool-King on display to the world, no one noticing the vacant pained stare of Juliano, answering for the decades of sins he'd accumulated. If that would be part of the Mardi Gras' reason for being, the indulgences before piety and sobriety were the manners of society.

"They'll be looking for any girl, when you think on it," she whispered back, "though I doubt they'll ever get the right to ask all of us to strip so they can see whose body was at the scene."

She didn't hear the laugh or giggle, knowing her partner would do his best not to draw attention. "So they saw everything of you."

"They saw nothing," she answered with another whisper. "but the mask I wore. And that's gone now."

She leaned forward, smiling through the red veil that was only part of her harlequin costume. She caught the attention of the waitress, nodding for a bottle of beer, then took off the veil and kept smiling through the concert and through the rest of her life.

Paul Wartenberg is a long-term Florida resident who has visited New Orleans on several occasions, but only as a designated driver. He's also familiar with the concept of Tampa's Gasparilla celebration, but nobody's invited him to one yet. He'll let you know when he gets that damned "first novel" finished. Maybe.

MR. SUGAR VS. THE CAKE THIEF
BY
MARIAN ALLEN

I'm not ashamed to say I got lonely for Mrs. DiMarco. After all, we were a good team. It isn't every day a neutered white Persian cat (myself) and a foul-mouthed cat-hater (Mrs. DiMarco) save the neighborhood from a Martian sampling team. And yet, we did.

After that, daily life loses some of its zest.

I'll be honest: daily life was still zesty until our neighbors moved, taking my unrequited beloved, Stallone, with them. Ah, me, what a lovely boy he was!

So, on a beautiful day in early spring, I catfooted down the block and across the street to Mrs. DiMarco's modest home.

By "modest," I mean, "not over-large." There's nothing shy or retiring about it. Mrs. DiMarco is one of those people who believe if one lawn ornament is good, ten lawn ornaments are ten times better. I had my choice of urinating on a pink flamingo, an albino lawn jockey, a gnome, a gazing ball, a birdbath shaped like a sunflower, a bird feeder shaped like a child with cupped hands, a ceramic turtle, or a rabbit with twinkling LED flowers around its neck. The statue of St. Francis and the Mary-in-a-bathtub shrine to the Blessed Virgin were, of course, safe; I consider myself a Catholic cat, since I eat fish every Friday. I eat fish every chance I get.

But today—today stopped me in my tracks. Today, festoons of metallic bunting in green, purple, and gold draped and wrapped every drapable and wrappable architectural element. Jester heads on sticks poked up along either side of the walk; I had no doubt they glowed in the dark. The flamingo, lawn jockey, gnome, birdseed child, turtle, and rabbit wore little

109

masks. St. Francis sported an admirable collection of green, purple, and gold beads. Only the Holy Mother of God stood pure, and I suspected no more than one DiMarco Manhattan had spared her.

The front door was wrapped in purple foil with yellow and purple letters scattered on it spelling out: "Laissez les bon temps roullez – Let the good times roll."

"Oh, God," I muttered, "is it Lent again already?"

Mardi Gras, actually; Fat Tuesday.

Mardi Gras means my humans have people over for a noisy party with lashings of food and drink.

Note the word Noisy. Not the word Food. Note the word Drink.

Feeling a bit bilious as I looked upon Mrs. DiMarco's tribute to drunken revelry, I wondered if I would be better off finding a sheltered spot indoors or outdoors. Indoors meant easy access to the food; outdoors meant no one would tread upon my tail.

The foil-covered door opened. I crouched, prepared to run if lying low failed to make me invisible. Mrs. DiMarco had a throwing arm that would be the envy of many a Major League pitcher, and an uncertain temper.

The screen door screeched, and the woman herself stepped onto the porch, carrying a broom and dustpan.

I won't describe her. She was human, so who cares what she looks like? My invisibility wish didn't work, because she saw me—she was amazingly perceptive, for a human—but she smiled.

"Weh-heh-hell, look who it ain't! Ragmop! What brings you down to the poor folks' end of the street?"

"To be honest," I said, "I missed you."

"Meow, meow, meow," she said. "Does that mean, 'Give me some food,' I wonder? Does it?"

"No," I said, "it doesn't. But, if you're offering, I wouldn't turn it down."

"Meow, meow," she said. "If you're still here when I get back, I'll give you some scrippy-scraps."

110

Humans. One can go through the wars with them, one can have a meeting of minds with them, one can understand every word they say, and the most one can hope for is that they'll be able to tell the difference between distress, anger, hunger, and joy by the tone of one's voice. True communication is beyond them.

Nevertheless, I purred as loudly as I could when she emptied a small storage dish into the grass (which, I probably needn't tell you, could have used a trim). Cold chicken is my second-favorite food, especially if it hasn't been picked over very well and still has a knot of gristle here and there. A man – even one who has been freed from the bondage of strictly masculine biology – likes something he can sink his teeth into.

While I enjoyed my al fresco repast, Mrs. DiMarco swept her porch, her steps, her walk, the sidewalk in front of her lawn, and the street in front of her property. It took her a little longer than it need have, since she kept dropping ash from the cigarette she never removed from the corner of her mouth and had to go back and sweep it up. It didn't seem to bother her, though, since she never stopped sweeping, smoking, nor singing "Oh, Lonesome Me" out of the side of her mouth not clamped on the cigarette.

From down the block, I heard my female human call into our back yard, "Sugar? Mr. Sugar! Kit-kit-kitty! Mr. Sugar!"

The pricking up of my ears must have betrayed me (I told you the woman is perceptive), because Mrs. DiMarco said, "Mr. Sugar? Is that your name, Ragmop? Mr. Sugar?" She took the cigarette from her mouth and laughed heartily, if hoarsely.

I affected not to notice. After cleaning my face, I left her yard and, stopping on the sidewalk to shake each of my rear paws in unmistakable insult, went home.

As I went, I saw what the garishness of Mrs. DiMarco's "decorations" had hitherto hidden from me: Every house had at least one purple-green-gold item displayed, and enticing aromas filled the air from every direction. Perhaps it would behoove me to actually listen to my humans and see if I could gather why.

When I reached the back porch, though, all I heard was Sweetheart (my female human) sobbing. Darling (my male human) made comforting noises, as well he should: She had

111

dumped a mess of half-burned and half-raw cake-like stuff into my outdoor food dish! Although I was the one in need of comforting, since it was my dish that had been so outraged, it was gratifying that Sweetheart was so sensitive to the injury she had done me.

"Don't worry, Sweetheart," Darling said, opening the back door and jingling his car keys. "I'll take care of it."

"It's too late! They'll be closing off the street in half an hour!"

It was, I conceded, probably not the state of my food dish, after all, that had her so upset.

"I'll be back in time with the goods." He hugged her. "Trust me."

"Be careful, Darling! Whoever killed that jewelry man is still at large."

"I'll lock the doors and stay far away from jewelry stores. I promise."

She dried her eyes, blew her nose, and closed the door behind him.

I used the cat flap to join her in the kitchen, where the smells of tomatoes, chicken, and spices overcame the stench of burned cake.

Sweetheart stirred something in a pot so large it could almost be called a cauldron. Oh, dear. This looked worse than a houseful of revelers. Big pot; closing the street; oh, dear. Block party.

I crept beneath the table, where I could keep an eye on interesting kitchen spills, resigned to another Mardi Gras in protective seclusion. How well I recalled my first Mardi Gras, before I knew it was best to hide away, when one of the guests carried me around under his chin, shouting, "Ho, ho, ho!" Did I mention that there was a great deal of intoxication involved in these parties?

By the time Darling returned, Sweetheart had divided a bottle of red wine between the pot and herself, and was singing "Let the Good Times Roll" in any number of keys.

Darling held up a blue and gold bag and trumpeted, "Ta daaaa! Got the last King Cake in town, I do believe. I had to go

112

all the way out to Lazy Glaze, and I had to do some mighty powerful salesmanship, but I talked the clerk out of this one. It was stuck behind the day-old donuts, but I found it. I told you to trust me!"

They did some of that disgusting mouth-mooshing that people do when they like one another, and Darling opened the cake box and another bottle of red wine.

The one good thing about a block party is that, weather permitting, they take place out-of-doors. The weather that day was beautiful, so Darling carried the pot Sweetheart had been stirring outside into the street. I followed them long enough to see that the street had been closed with sawhorses, and long tables had been set up on the lawns. Everyone wore a mask. Everyone wore a costume. Everyone wandered-- or, more properly speaking, caroused--from yard to yard, sharing food and liquid refreshment.

Mrs. DiMarco's distinctive rasp sawed through the air. I retreated to the back, through the cat door, and under the table. She was still audible, laughing until she had a coughing fit, listening to Sweetheart's saccharine tales of my kittenhood, no doubt.

I was so fixed on determining the cause of her amusement, I didn't hear the back door open until the hinges gave their tell-tale squeak.

Now, this was interesting. Why would anyone come in the back, when it was obvious everybody was in the street? He wore casual clothing and a purple-and-gold mask with a smile made into it. He slipped into the kitchen, casting glances around and over his shoulder, like a stray cat intent on raiding my food dish. A human prowler! I had never seen one of those before.

But the food was outside! I almost told him so, but he can't have failed to know it. Therefore, he was after something other than food. I prepared to follow him and add to my knowledge of human behavior, but he didn't leave the kitchen, so I stayed hidden.

He looked in the pantry and all the cabinets. He opened the oven and peered in. Apparently, what he wanted was not in any of those places, for he muttered curses every time he closed a place he had opened without success. When all else failed, he looked in the microwave, where Sweetheart had put the boxed King Cake so I wouldn't claw open the laughably flimsy container and sample it.

"Ah!"

He slid a knife out of the knife block and cut a wedge out of the cake. He was terribly careful: more careful than Darling, when Sweetheart has forbidden him to have another piece, and he cuts one at midnight, trying to strike a balance between what will satisfy him and what she won't notice.

The intruder carried the piece to the sink, where he crumbled it to bits. He cursed again and cut another slice. As he carried this second helping to the sink, something fell to the floor with a small clatter. It sparkled! Jewelry! A sparkly bracelet, in fact.

I didn't know why there was jewelry in the cake, but all jewelry in our house belongs to Sweetheart. Possibly, Darling had bought the jewelry as a special surprise for her and had it baked into the King Cake. At any rate, it didn't belong to this… this… person.

The masked intruder, cake box in hand, slipped out the back door. He was stealing Sweetheart's bracelet! And, more importantly, her cake! After Darling had made a special trip to get it! This was the outside of enough!

I followed him. He dumped the box into a metal basket on the front of a bicycle, hopped onto the seat, and shoved off. And I jumped on. Not on the seat, of course; on him.

He was game; I'll give him that. Most people would have stopped to thrash, if a cat had suddenly attached itself to them, all claws engaged. The thief, though, kept pedaling, although his mouth must have been stretched wide behind his mask, judging from the howl coming out of him. It rivaled the furious yowl coming from my own mouth as I protested.

"Stop! Thief!" This was the first thing I shouted, closely followed by, "At least slow down, so I can get off! Cat in distress! Help! Help!"

The alley dead-ended at the back of someone's garage, so the thief turned left, bumping over the tree roots and fallen branches of a poorly-groomed back yard and out onto the street. Weaving in and out amongst the merrymakers, he headed for the crossroad, where he could disappear into the traffic beyond.

Suddenly, we were airborne! Up we went in an acrobatic arc. We landed with a *whump* on a patch of grass, narrowly missing having our eyes poked out by the pious fingers of St. Francis. The thief, I'm happy to say, landed on this belly, which meant I was safely on his back. After catching my breath, I detached myself from him, taking care not to break a claw. While he gasped to recover some of the air the fall had knocked out of him, I looked around for the aerodynamic bike. It lay in the street, surrounded by revelers in various states of intoxication, its spokes deformed by the broom handle shoved through them.

The cake box had fallen and broken open, and bright stones glittered in the streetlights.

A familiar voice brayed, "DAY-yum! I just solved the Davis heist! Call the cops! Dibs on the reward!" Mrs. DiMarco bent over and sneered into the cake thief's face. "Try to take off with my pal, Ragmop, will ya? Guess you didn't know he was part of a mighty crime-fighting team, did ya? Guess you'll think twice about tangling with Ragmop and DiMarco again, won't ya? Catnappin' so-and-so." Only she didn't say "so-and-so."

By the time the police arrived, the cake thief was ready to waive his rights and confess. He worked at the bakery, but was also a jewel thief. He baked his takings into cakes and pies, marked the boxes, and sold the loaded pastries to confederates. This particular cake had been filled with the goods from the Davis Diamonds robbery. Darling, finding no King Cakes in the store, had waited until the innocent girl behind the counter had gone into the back, and had dug out one (marked and loaded, unknown to him) from behind the day-old donuts. When she had returned, he had flourished his find, charged it, and brought it home. The thief had gotten our address from the charge slip and had come to reclaim his stolen goods.

He hadn't reckoned with me. Or, I admit it freely, with Mrs. DiMarco.

The time may come when I've had enough chicken and salmon as rewards, and when I become weary of praise, petting, photographs for the paper and magazines (not to mention internet memes), but that time has not yet come.

I'm even beginning to develop a slight fondness for being called Ragmop. But only when Mrs. DiMarco does it.

Marian Allen was born in Louisville, Kentucky and now lives in rural Indiana. For as long as she can remember, she has loved telling and being told stories. She writes science fiction, fantasy, mystery, humor, horror, mainstream, and anything else she can wrestle into fixed form.

Allen has had stories in on-line and print publications, on coffee cans and the wall of an Indian restaurant in Louisville, Kentucky. Her latest books are the SAGE *fantasy trilogy and her science fiction novel* Sideshow in the Center Ring *from Three Fates Press.*

She is a member of Quills and Quibbles and the Southern Indiana Writers Group.

Allen has worked as a high school teacher, an executive secretary, an accountant, and in Red Cross Youth Services. She is married, with three step/adopted daughters and one birth daughter. She is active in the Friends of Harrison County Library, Woman's Literary Club of Corydon and Community Unity, which promotes diversity appreciation and non-violent problem solving.

She has pages on Facebook, Twitter, Goodreads, Google+ and LinkedIn and she posts at the group blog Fatal Foodies *on Tuesdays and monthly on* The Write Type.

In addition to writing, she is one of the administrators of Three Fates Press.

TWICE WIDOWED
BY
B.B. ANDERS

Chapter One

Dr. Brag leaned back in his chair, balancing a yellow legal pad on his crossed legs. He reminded me of my father, but only on the surface. There was something cold in the doctor's face. He was the textbook picture of a psychiatrist: deep brown eyes, plastic smile, and a neatly trimmed white beard. Still, 'Doctor Brag' was hardly a name to instill confidence in patients. Who wanted to tell all their most intimate secrets to Dr. 'Brag'?

I certainly didn't.

He just sat there watching me, watching him.

We'd been like this for the last ten minutes. His eyes hadn't left me since they brought me to this hell-hole. He watched and smiled.

I sulked, waited, and wondered if he was going to do anything but flash that same vapid smile that was plastered on every face in this place.

Jason might think these clean white walls and antiseptic rooms were better than prison, but he was wrong. This institution was just another kind of prison. At least in prison I wouldn't be surrounded by drug-induced stupidity.

Maybe the stupidity wasn't induced. Last night they served a plain white cake with purple, gold, and green frosting and these fools in the ward didn't even realize that putting little sugar baby dolls on every cube did not make it a King Cake. That didn't matter though; at least this year I wouldn't have to kill Jason's date.

"Is there anything you would like to say?" Brag finally asked.

"Not really."

"I see," he said, scribbling something onto his yellow pad. He noticed my eyes following his pen and smiled. "Would you like to see?"

Did he honestly just ask me that? *What kind of game is he playing?*

"I thought my records were confidential." I said aloud.

"They're your records," he replied. "You should be allowed to look at them, shouldn't you? You can look at anything I write, if you want."

I started to lean forward, and then I realized this was a calculated trick to get me to trust him. He wanted me to think I had some control of the situation. That wasn't going to work on me. I slouched back in the big leather armchair and continued watching him.

He frowned. At last, a genuine emotion, the first I'd seen in this place.

Dr. Brag sat up in his chair and regarded me for a moment. "Why?" he asked.

I had no intention of telling him that I refused to play his games. There was only one reason he kept me in this place. He thought I was crazy.

He was not to be trusted. Anything I said to him would be twisted into a weapon he could use against me. So I said nothing. I left his question hanging and retreated back inside my own head. That was the only safe place.

He sat there watching me for what seemed like an eternity. Since we only had an hour, twenty minutes of which was already gone, the silence couldn't have lasted more than fifteen minutes, tops. Then he got up, walked to the bookcase, picked up a fluffy little white lamb, and tossed it into my lap.

"What's this thing for?" What did he expect me to do with the creature? I had no use for children's toys.

He took his seat again. This time he left the pad and pencil on his desk. "That was my daughter's favorite toy."

"What do you want me to do with it?"

"Nothing," he said. "You remind me of her."

There was something cold in the way he spoke. I sensed a trap, but he had piqued my curiosity.

"How?" I asked.

"She always needed something secure to hang on to when she was about to cry."

"I'm not about to cry."

"When she was alone."

"You're here," I said, "and the nurses, and the orderlies, and everyone else charged with watching the crazies. I'm never alone."

"You're not crazy."

"Of course not," I said, tightening my grip on the lamb's neck. "You keep me locked up here because there's absolutely nothing wrong with me."

"How about because you're angry?"

He had me there. I was angry. Why shouldn't I be angry? That cheating Jason had me locked up here while he was out chasing other women.

Dr. Brag was watching me again, gauging my reaction to the thought of being angry.

"What was her name?" I asked.

"Who?"

"Your daughter. You said the lamb belonged to her."

Dr. Brag's steady gaze made me feel like I was being dissected. "I thought you knew her name. It was Anna."

"Doesn't Anna want her lamb anymore?"

"She's dead."

"Oh."

"I think our time is up," he said.

"Can I keep the lamb?"

"Of course," he said, the plastic smile back in place.

My knuckles were whiter than the fleece on the lamb's neck they gripped. He thought he was winning. He was wrong.

Chapter Two

Jason Hoffman had heard enough.

"Dr. Brag, why are you bothering me about her? She isn't part of my life anymore. She's in your hospital for a reason. I trust you. I don't need a blow by blow account of your sessions. I don't even need to be reminded that she is there. Just take care of her and leave me alone."

"Mr. Hoffman, please, your involvement is important to her recovery."

Recovery. Jason was appalled at the thought.

"She isn't going to recover, Doctor. She stabbed a woman to death on my sofa!"

Jason reined in his emotions before they got the better of him again. He wished he could tell Dr. Brag that he never thought about his ex, never woke up in the middle of the night soaked in cold sweat, never saw the blood or lifted that feathered Mardi Gras mask and looked into dead eyes.

He couldn't lie. She had been a big part of his life, even after the murder. That's why he had helped get her into a real hospital instead of the state one. It had taken every bit of his legal skill to keep her out of one of those awful wards where she would have lived out her life drugged to the gills surrounded by maniacs. Maybe she deserved that.

"Doctor, my ex is bat-shit crazy. If I had known when we met how one loony woman could mess up my life, I would have sworn off women forever."

"You didn't swear off women, did you, Mr. Hoffman? You married her. Legally, you are still her husband. Don't you think you have an obligation to see this through?"

"We'd been separated for ten months before the murder, Doctor. I would divorce her in a heartbeat if it weren't for the health insurance. You don't think I could afford your facility without insurance, do you?"

"Why should that matter? If you believe she is not your problem, why not leave her future to the state?"

"She doesn't have a future. She's a crazy killer. You didn't see what she did to that woman. You didn't look at those grotesque stab wounds or see the blood."

Jason knew he was yelling. He didn't care. Both their lives had turned to crap the moment she picked up that knife. Everything after that was one unending nightmare.

Here it was, the middle of Mardi Gras season. He should be out attending the fêtes and enjoying life. She had taken that away from him. Because of her, Mardi Gras was ruined and Dr. Brag thought his wife should be let out where she could kill again. The thought made him so sick, he was thinking of moving out of Louisiana. He could pass the bar up North, somewhere far away from parades and parties.

Chapter Three

Why do I keep trying to twist the head off this poor little lamb?

Oh God! It makes me think of her, innocent, big, blue eyes, a soft, helpless, little thing. Why did she have to get in the way?

None of this would have happened if she hadn't got between me and Jason. I could have won him back, made him love me again. Then I wouldn't be in this hell-hole. I wouldn't be here waiting for the therapist to see me, to try to find my deep-rooted psychological problem. The only problem I have is that Jason is out there and probably finding another sweet young thing to replace me with. Like he ever could replace me; we're soul mates. Jason and I belong together. Deep down, he knows that.

"The doctor will see you now."

"What?"

Disoriented, I stare at the receptionist behind the window.

"Dr. Brag is waiting," she says sweetly, pointing to the door as she presses the buzzer.

"Oh yeah," I say, as I get up to go sit in his office and watch his professional stare for the next hour.

We went through the usual preliminaries. He smiled his plastic smile. I hunched in my chair and weighed each word out of his mouth before responding.

"I see you are still carrying the lamb."

"Thought you might like to see it," I replied. "Being your daughter's and all."

Dr. Brag looked down at my white knuckles but didn't say anything about the grip I had on the lamb's neck. He didn't have to. The way he looked at me was enough to make me loosen my hold, at least for a moment.

"Have you spoken to your husband since you arrived?"

That was a low blow. He knew that Jason was the one who tracked me down and arranged for me to be brought me here. Not that he'd had anything to do with me since. He hadn't even had the decency to tell me that he was behind getting me out of the state mental hospital, but there wasn't anyone else who would have. Jason had seen to that. He took me far away from everyone who cared. He was all I had. Then he didn't want me.

"He doesn't want to talk to me."

"How does that make you feel?"

Why was he pressing me to talk about Jason?

I looked around the room, searching for something to distract him.

"Why are all the walls painted white?" I asked.

"White is a calming color."

"White isn't a color at all," I countered.

Secretly, I was considering what it meant to have all the walls painted white. White to keep us calm, evidently sanity was white, clean, boring. Sanity wasn't at all like the colors of Mardi Gras, dazzling shades of gold, green, purple, and red...so much red. She didn't want to think about the red. That was all Jason's fault.

They had painted an entire institution full of insane people the non-color of sanity. Why on earth would anyone do that, unless they were twisted? That made sense. The people running the show were as twisted as the freak show residing in the wards. The staff probably dipped into the drugs as well.

122

For some reason, thinking about the white walls got me to my feet. I could feel his eyes following me as I paced around the room.

I didn't like this room, didn't like the calming white or the smell of too many candles. It reminded me of the room where my mother practiced yoga. I hated that room.

There was a jar candle burning on the table. Why hadn't I ever noticed that before? I passed my fingers through the flame. The flame was good; clean…I liked the burn.

"What are you doing?" Dr. Brag asked.

"Enticing the flame out of hiding."

"Why should a flame hide?"

"Because it is afraid to show what it really is," I said.

He studied me until his attempt to get under my skin, inside my brain, made me shudder.

"Is that what you did?" he said, so softly that the words bounced off my body.

"Why would I hide? I know what I am. The whole world knows what I am. I have no reason to hide."

"What exactly are you?" he asked in that same soft voice.

"A person who knows what she wants. Someone who won't stop until she has it."

"Is that all?"

"You have my chart," I shouted. "Why don't you tell me?"

"All your records tell me is that you killed an innocent woman."

Anger flared up from deep inside me. "She wasn't innocent; she was a lying witch out to steal my husband."

"Is that what you tell yourself?"

I glared at him. "Maybe."

"She didn't do anything to you. I've read the reports. She just came to a Mardi Gras party and hooked up with an attractive man. You killed her. Did you even know her?"

"I knew her."

"What did you know? You've told me she was on a date with your ex," he said.

"He is not my ex *anything*. We are still married. He is mine."

"No he isn't," Dr. Brag insisted. "We don't own the people we love, not even our spouses or children. No piece of paper gives you ownership of another person."

"Jason is mine. She had no right to try to take him from me. I should have cut her more. She needed to suffer more. I should have laughed while she was bleeding, and cut her while she begged for mercy."

Tears were rolling down my cheeks, but I didn't care. I had to make him understand. My fist pounded the table, struck the jar candle. Glass and hot wax mingled with my blood, dripped into a red and yellow swirl onto the table top. Then the nurse came to sedate me.

Dr. Brag stood there watching. Something in his eyes nagged me, but my brain wasn't able to grasp what I saw.

At least there are real colors left in the world, I thought, looking down at the swirl of colors on Dr. Brag's desk as the medicine took hold.

Chapter Four

The moment his assistant uttered Dr. Brag's name, Jason grabbed the phone.

"Mr. Hoffman."

"What is it?" Jason asked. "I thought I made it clear that I didn't want to hear from you."

"I think it is time you came to one of your wife's sessions."

"God! Is that necessary?"

"I believe we are close to unlocking the truth. Your presence at our next meeting could trigger a breakthrough."

Jason's disgust was evident in his voice.

"Where did you come up with the cockamamie idea that putting the two of us in the same room would help anyone?"

"Everything you have told me indicates you were the motivation for her crime. You could also be the one person who can bring reality back."

"You are wasting your time. Get it through your head, Dr. Brag. My wife is incurable. She lost her mind and stabbed a woman to death in the middle of our living room."

"What makes you say that?"

"Look Doc, you're not going to get inside her head. She's too smart to let you do that. Even if you could, what makes you think it's a good idea? Two minutes inside that messed-up mind of hers could drive a man as insane as she is."

"Your wife is not insane."

"Yeah, and I'm going to win the lottery without ever buying a ticket."

Silence filled the void.

"Look Dr. Brag, stop trying to fix her. She isn't worth the effort. All I need you to do is keep her calm and locked up where she can't hurt anyone else."

Jason hung up the phone.

He sat there thinking about Dr. Brag's stupid theory for the next hour. What if he was right? The more he told himself it was a stupid idea, the more he wondered if it was possible to get through the crazy and find out the truth about what happened that night. Maybe he was as crazy as his wife. He picked up the phone and called her doctor back.

Chapter Five

"I've invited Jason to our next session," Dr. Brag said.

"It doesn't matter. He won't come."

"What makes you say that?"

Her hands tightened on the lamb.

"If Jason cared, he would have come to see me before now."

The expression in his eyes told her she had hit the mark. Jason didn't care.

"He says that, if he can get away from the office, he'll come."

"That means he won't come," she said, twisting the toy in her hands. "Jason cares about making money, not about me."

"He might surprise you. Why don't we just wait and see?"

125

"I tell you he doesn't care. He hasn't cared about me in years. That's why he made me put up with his endless parade of lovers. Do you think that last year's fling was the first?"

"Why stay with him?"

"Because he is mine and I would rather die than give him up. Does that sound crazy, doctor?"

"What do you think?"

"I think that he didn't care any more about them than he did me. Jason loves Jason. He might have loved me once, in the beginning. I'm not sure if he really loved me or if he only loved what I represented. But I loved him, even when he used me as a trophy on his arm. Jason worked his way through law school as a mechanic. He wanted someone with more sophistication than he had. I was the right someone to help him get ahead. He loved me for that, maybe he loved me for myself too, in the beginning."

"And the other women?"

I didn't like the way Dr. Brag was looking at me. Waiting, what was he waiting for me to say? That Jason used women for sex, for social climbing, for whatever they could give him.

"They have no right to him," I said. "None. That witch thought she could take him away from me. She was taunting me with their sordid little affair."

"Taunting you, all the way from Chicago? How? Wasn't she just a tourist who stumbled into the wrong party?"

I clutched the lamb as if my life depended on holding onto the squishy piece of fluff between my fingers.

"Jason had no secrets from me," I said, unable to suppress the bitterness in my voice. "He thought he was clever, keeping his infidelity to women from other towns, but I always knew. I could smell them on his skin when he came home, taste them in his kisses."

"How did that make you feel?"

How did that make me feel? Did I feel? I didn't know anymore. Everything was dark, black, empty…

126

Chapter Six

Gumbo sat like a rock in Jason's stomach. He should have skipped lunch. Twice he had picked up the phone to tell Dr. Brag he wasn't coming. Why should he? He didn't owe her anything. He could cancel and not give the appointment a second thought.

He didn't cancel.

At one o'clock sharp, he walked through Dr. Brag's door and made his way through the lobby to a safety-glassed reception window.

A middle-aged matron with sharp features and a slightly crooked nose greeted him.

"Jason Hoffman to see Dr. Brag," he said to the receptionist. "He's expecting me."

She pressed a buzzer and the door unlocked.

"Go right in, Mr. Hoffman. The doctor is waiting."

The woman's disapproving gaze reminded Jason of his sixth grade teacher. The old bat always looked at him like he was a piece of filth that wandered in by mistake. He was doing Dr. Brag a favor by coming to one of his wife's sessions. So what if he had cheated a little on his marriage vows? *She* was the murderer. That was a lot worse than having a little something on the side.

Jason took a seat in one of the leather armchairs across from the doctor. His foot tapped out a nervous rhythm on the floor as he waited. He didn't know if he was crazy or stupid for being in Dr. Brag's office. The thought of seeing her again pushed his anxiety to the limits.

There was something that didn't sit right about Dr. Brag, either. Seeing him was almost as creepy as being in a locked room with her. It was all he could do to keep from bolting out of the office.

Chapter Seven

I wasn't eager to see Dr. Brag, not that I believed for a moment Jason would be there, but the fact that he had been invited made the walk to his office nerve-racking. It didn't help

127

that the gorilla escorting me alternated between popping his gum and giving me one of those plastic smiles that is supposed to be reassuring. All I could do was ignore him as I placed one foot in front of the other.

Something was different, something I couldn't put my finger on. I hesitated outside the door until the door relocked. Dr. Brag's receptionist had to buzz me in a second time before I built up enough nerve to open the door.

There were two heads instead of one.

What was this, another doctor to try to shrink my brain back into my head? Lots of luck with that.

"I have a surprise for you," Dr. Brag said.

He gave me another vapid smile and waved to the other chair. "Is there something you would like to say to Jason?"

Jason's head, but it couldn't be him. What was Jason doing here?

"What's he doing here?" I sputtered. "I don't want to see him."

"I wanted to see how you would react to talking to Jason. Don't you think it's time to settle things between you?"

"Do you want a blood bath?" I asked. "I don't think your carpets are stain-proof."

"There's not going to be a blood bath," Dr. Brag said. "Nobody is going to harm anyone in this office."

There was a long pause while she looked at her husband's face. There was something wrong. It was Jason's face, but it wasn't Jason. It couldn't be. Jason wouldn't be here...

"She couldn't hit me if she tried." Jason said.

I leapt from my seat.

"Don't be so sure of yourself," I said, glaring at him. "I'll take you out just like I did your girlfriend."

"You and what army?" he yelled.

Dr. Brag cleared his throat. "Boys and girls, take a seat and play nice together."

"He started it," I grumbled, sinking into the nearest chair.

"Grow up," Jason said.

"I didn't ask you to come here."

"He did," Jason said, pointing across the desk where Dr. Brag sat scribbling in his yellow pad.

At that moment I was more certain than ever that Dr. Brag was not to be trusted.

"You are part of each other's lives, whether either of you want to acknowledge that or not. Everything that happened is intertwined. It is time that you resolve what's at the root of your problem."

"How do you propose we do that, Doctor?" Jason asked.

"Get real, Jason, I don't know what he's talking about and neither do you. You're nothing, less than nothing, to me."

"You don't want to know," Dr. Brag said, "but you know. Deep down you know exactly what part you play in Jason's life. Everyone in this room knows, and it is time for the truth to come out."

"Jason's life? I thought this was all about me."

"You think everything is about you," Jason said. "You still want to be the spoiled little daddy's girl I married. Well, Daddy can't get you out of this one, sweetheart. You left him behind the day you married me."

Dr. Brag smiled, not the vapid plastic smile he used in his therapy sessions, this was a real smile, a sinister wicked one like those on movie villains when they finally have the hero.

"I've arranged a little field trip to the cemetery. It is time the two of you confront the truth."

"Look, Dr. Brag," Jason said, "I've had enough of your game. I cleared my schedule for an hour to come to this session, but I'm not going to go on any field trips. Certainly not to some creepy cemetery full of live oaks and Spanish moss with *her*. The two of you can fight mosquitoes on your own."

"You agreed to help."

"Doctor, I'm telling you she's a lost cause; everyone's forgotten about her. Why can't you just keep her here where she can't hurt anyone else?"

"Pain can't remain hidden away forever. We are all going," Dr. Brag said firmly. "It is essential to face the truth before any healing can take place. Please, Mr. Hoffman, don't make this more difficult."

Incredulity registered in Jason's face, but when Dr. Brag buzzed for the orderlies, he got up and followed them to the institutions waiting van.

Chapter Eight

"I don't need this," I said.

"Don't you want to know the reason?"

I stopped mid-step and spun around so fast that the orderlies didn't have time to keep me out of Dr. Brag's face. "Reason? Is that what this is about? If that's all you want, I'll tell you both the reason."

Jason was looking at me. His eyes pleaded with me to stop, but I didn't care. Jason used me, then tried to throw me away. He deserved to hear the truth.

"I killed her because I hated her. Hated her, do you understand?" The goons were holding my arms so I couldn't strike out at the doctor, but they couldn't hold back what I had to say. "She took the person I loved most from me, and didn't even have the guts to tell me she was sorry."

"Don't look at me like that, Jason. Sure I hated her--and I killed her, but don't stand there judging me. It wouldn't have happened if it hadn't been for you. That's right Jason. You."

Chapter Nine

"Do you hear that, Doctor? I told you my coming here was a waste of time. She is never going to grow up and take responsibility for what she's done. All she wants to do is blame me."

Chapter Ten

"Get in the van, Jason," Dr. Brag said.

"Get in the van, Jason," I echoed.

"Shut up," Jason said. "I don't even know you anymore. Maybe I never did."

"Oh, you know me. I've been covering your mistakes for years. No more, Jason. Now it is time to pay up for all the crap you unloaded on me."

"What's that supposed to mean?"

"I didn't want to kill her, Jason. The whole time I was stabbing her I could feel my hands getting weaker and weaker. You kept them going, Jason. You made me stab her…stab her again and again."

"You're crazy. You don't know what you're talking about," Jason said, his voice rising higher with each word.

"Yes you do," I said, reveling in the fear I saw in his face. "You know everything, Jason."

Chapter Eleven

"We're here," Dr. Brag said, as the van pulled through the cemetery gates.

The bickering in the back seat stopped. Jason Hoffman felt a cold chill run the length of his body. He didn't want to look, but couldn't help himself.

"That's right, Jason," Dr. Brag said. "You know where we're going."

He turned to the orderly beside him.

"I'd like to offer Mr. Hoffman some privacy. If you could stand a little distance away during our visit, I would appreciate it."

Chapter Twelve

"Say something," Jason screamed at me.

I smiled that same angelic smile I had given him on our wedding day. He knew the truth now. He couldn't turn away. I had killed her, deliberately, killed her because I loved him, because he couldn't keep it in his pants.

Jason sobbed. Great crocodile tears rolled down his face as the orderly led him to the graveside, then moved a short distance away. He didn't need to be led. Jason hadn't visited here since the funeral, but he knew every step of the way by heart. He had finally come to see me.

The wind bit to the bone on that walk.

I walked along beside him, watching him cry. I didn't hurt now, didn't hate. I smiled at him again, then slowly dissolved into the nothingness he had made of us.

Chapter Thirteen

Jason Hoffman stood looking down at the black marble stone, looking into the blackness of his own soul as he read the familiar words:

Anne Marie Brag-Hoffman
Born April 3, 1978
Died February 16, 1999

He stared at Anne's grave. What he saw were all eight of those beautiful young women he seduced, then turned to Anne to kill. She had hated them, killed them for his sake, just like she had killed herself. Had her maiden name been Brag? Where had that memory gone? Had *she* stolen it?

"Anne please, tell them it wasn't me."

"But it was you, Jason," Dr. Brag said. "You know that now. And for the rest of your miserable life you are going to know that you killed my Anne. You killed her, as surely as if you had wielded the knife with your own hand. The coroner called it suicide, but it was you. Trouble was, you couldn't be free of her."

Jason's eyes pleaded for him to stop.

"Every Mardi Gras, you kill another woman. Never again, Jason. I anonymously helped the police chase you down. When you retreated into madness, blamed Anne for your murders, they put you in the state hospital. I couldn't allow it to go at that."

In the state hospital? *Him?* No, he had an office. A white office with a high window.

Dr. Brag moved inches from Jason's face.

"You don't get to hide behind memories of my little girl. I won't let you."

132

Jason's knees weakened.

"You shouldn't have eloped, Jason. I got you moved to Lafayette, got you put in my care. Nobody at the hospital knew I was your father-in-law. Even you. If you told them now, who would believe you?"

That wicked, sinister smile of his was back on Dr. Brag's face.

"Anne is all the way gone now. You took her from me and I have taken her from you. You can't escape into being my little girl anymore. This is all you. The murders, all those women you killed. It was you Jason. The only person Anne ever hurt was herself, and you drove her to that. Now you get to live with what you've done. I'm going to keep you in my hospital for the rest of your stinking life. You're never going to get the chance to take Anne's way out. And every day I'm going to be there to remind you of what a murdering little asswipe you are."

B.B. Anders is not a mental health professional, but she has needed one from time to time. Fortunately, she lives in the Tampa Bay area, where she is one grain of sand on a big wacky beach. This is her first published story.

VOODOO HONEYMOON
BY
LANCE ZARIMBA

It was Jon's idea to go to New Orleans after our wedding, but it was I who planned our honeymoon to fall during Mardi Gras, and it was in full swing. Bourbon Street was littered with half naked sweaty bodies, beads, beer, and babes. Seeing the shirtless men made my heart race and certain other parts swell, as the drinks flowed easily and Zydeco music filled the air.

"Are you having fun?" my new husband, Jon, yelled to me. He carried a bright pink Hurricane in a three foot long glass with an even longer straw. His cheeks were red from all of the alcohol and exertion. Strands of plastic beads hung around his neck, and his shirt was wide open showing his hairy sculpted chest. His wonderful treasure trail disappeared into his bulging shorts. The hair on his tan legs was matted down from sweat. He was sockless and wore brand new white sneakers. He flipped his black, wavy hair away from his face and smiled.

I clinked my beer bottle to his glass. "This is great. I'm so glad we did this." My blond hair was damp, more from other people's sweat than my own. I pushed someone out of my way and moved closer to Jon as we tried to move down the crowded sidewalk. We passed bars, restaurants, voodoo shops, and T-shirt stores. The French Quarter in New Orleans appeared to be almost back to its old glory after Hurricane Katrina had done her worst.

"I'm hungry," I shouted to him as we passed by Marie Laveau's House of Voodoo.

"You're always hungry," he said. He faced me and kissed me hard, rubbing his erection against mine. He still was the hottest man alive.

"With all that alcohol," I pointed to his glass, "I'm sure you're not, but …" my hand cupped his arousal.

"Yeah, yeah, yeah. Let's find a nice place to eat. Jambalaya sounds great or a shrimp po' boy." He lifted his empty glass. "I think I need a refill."

Bayou Burger loomed to our right and as we neared the front door, several tables appeared open.

As we entered the restaurant, a man with his head painted black and a white skull painted over that nodded to us. "Young lovers," his deep rich voice said, drawing us to his makeshift table.

We stepped closer, thinking he was the host.

He pulled out a rusty pair of scissors from nowhere, snipped a lock of blond hair from my head, and turned to get a curl from Jon. His long bony fingers tied the locks of blond and black hair into two small tufts and made small little male dolls with bones, sticks and red ribbon. He held them up in front of us to see them.

My doll seemed to glow in the dark light. My body tingled all over, making the hair on my body stand on end.

His skeletal mouth spread into a wide grin and the dolls disappeared.

His black soulless eye sockets looked at us and rushed out into the street. A white business card floated out of his pocket and landed on the floor at our feet.

I bent over and picked it up. It was blank on both sides.

The real Bayou Burger host greeted us with huge menus and whisked us off to a table. "Your waiter will be with you shortly." She snapped her fingers, and a man carried two glasses of ice water to us.

As I turned to thank her, she was gone. I blinked my eyes.

"What was on the card?" Jon asked.

I handed it to him.

He flipped the card over and over. "What the hell was that all about? Was that crazy or what? Made me tingle all over, felt like lightning struck me, and I think I came a little bit in my shorts."

I knew what he meant. "I felt that too."

His hairy leg rubbed against mine under the table, and I applied pressure to his. "I thought for sure he was going to hit us up for a twenty or something. Our own personal voodoo dolls." I laughed, but a strange feeling fell over my body.

Jon handed the card back to me, and I slipped it into my back pocket. I picked up my menu and scanned the choices. Everything looked so good. I wanted to try everything on it.

The waiter appeared with a fresh Hurricane and an ice-cold Bud, just like what we had been drinking. I didn't remember ordering anything yet, or hearing Jon do the same. "What can I get for you?" he asked, as he set the Hurricane in front of Jon and the beer in front of me.

The party in the street raged on as I agonized over what to order. I looked up and out the window into the street. The voodoo doll man held Jon's doll and waved his hand in front of the doll and motioned to follow.

A bell rang in the back of the restaurant from the kitchen and the waiter said, "I'll be right back." He closed his order pad and hurried to the back.

Jon looked straight ahead and slowly rose to his feet. He walked past me without saying a word and continued out into the street of partiers.

"Jon? Jon." I called, but he continued down the street.

I pulled out my wallet, threw a twenty on the table, and raced after Jon.

Jon hadn't waited for me, and I frantically scanned the crowd for him. I spotted his black curls in the distance as he continued walking in the daze. He turned at a corner and headed down a side street.

I pushed my way between partiers and tried to keep him in sight. The side street wasn't as busy, but drunks staggered along the alley. I dodged trash cans filled with empty bottles and discarded beads across the bricks in the street.

"Jon," I called, but he continued walking. I spotted the voodoo man several blocks away, still moving his fingers in front of the doll.

"Excuse me," a drunken blonde tripped into my arms.

I caught her and prevented her from falling only to swing her around to keep her up right. Her tube top was very tight and many strands of beads hung around her neck.

"Do you want some beads?" she slurred.

I looked over her shoulder and Jon was further away. I pressed her back against the garbage can and held her there. "Stay," was all I said.

Her hand rose to her beads and started to lift one off.

I turned and rushed after Jon.

"Hey, don't you want my beads?" she called to my back.

My foot slipped in a puddle on the bricks and I went down to my hands and knees. My hands and knees stung from the road rash. I pushed up and looked down the alley.

Jon was gone.

I ran to the corner and looked both ways, no Jon. I ran the next block and turned the corner where the voodoo man once stood.

Another Dixieland band played happy music as the drunks staggered around. I scanned the crowd and didn't see Jon or the voodoo man. I slipped my hand into my back pocket and felt the business card. I pulled it out and looked at. The blood from my palm sucked into the card and words with strange symbols slowly appeared as the blood entered and filled the card.

Rev. Necro Mancer, 1265 Esplanade Avenue, New Orleans, 1 – 888 - THE – DEAD

Jon was gone, but I had an idea of where he was heading. I raced to the corner in search of a taxi.

I looked at the street sign as the cab driver stopped. I handed him a twenty and stepped onto Esplanade Avenue. 1263 was on the next block. I counted the buildings as I ran by the homes. 1261 was the Storyville Hotel, and next door was 1265. I knew I was getting close. A huge pink two-story square house rose up from the street and filled the block. Four white columns opened onto a porch with a balcony above.

I hurried down the street and frantically looked for Jon. Why was he acting so strange? Could he really be under the influence of voodoo? That wasn't real. Or was it? I always thought it was something the locals did to entertain the tourists, but this was scary.

The buildings were turning into more residential than business, as I hurried down the street. As I looked at the front door, Jon disappeared inside a pink home with pillars and a porch that wrapped around the front and side of the building. A wrought iron speared fence surrounded the yard.

I pulled on the iron gate and tried to get it to open. The rusty metal screamed in protest.

The door closed, and he was gone.

I pulled the gate far enough to enter and left it gaping open. I ran up the stairs and pulled on the doorknob. It was unlocked, and I entered. "Jon? Jon. Jon!" I yelled. I didn't care if anyone knew I was there.

The living room looked as if I had stepped back in time. Overstuffed furniture, huge portraits, and life-size sculptures filled the room. A thick Persian carpet covered parquet floor. The room opened up into a sun room off the back of the house with a beautiful southern exposure. A formal dining room ready for guests and waited in the other direction. A chair was tipped over on its back in the dining room and I headed in that direction. I pushed the swing door open to peek into the kitchen. An old white enameled stove dominated the room, but no Jon.

A thud came from upstairs, and I headed back to living room and found the staircase going up. I crept up the wooden stairs and watched between the spindles that held the hand railing to the staircase.

No one was in the hallway.

Four closed doors lined the upper floor and the lush wallpaper told of wealth and times gone by. I opened the closest door and found a dusty bedroom. Further down the hall was another bedroom, frilly and pink with lace curtains and a dressing table of crystal bottles and perfume. The scent of lavender and jasmine hung in the musty air of the room.

At the front of the house, the next door waited. I opened it slowly, and saw Jon standing with his back to me. He faced a chair with a high back. The voodoo man sat holding both of our voodoo dolls. A fire burned in the small fireplace next to him.

As my eyes adjusted to the darker room, I saw rows and rows of voodoo dolls that lined the room. Small ones, big ones, old, ugly, cute, bright, funny, and scary.

"He is mine now," the man said.

"What?" I asked.

"Your man is my man," he said.

I looked around the room and felt all the eyes of the dolls, even the ones with empty sockets, looking at me. I touched Jon's back. He felt cold to the touch, his body didn't react to my touch. Usually, he was warm and soft and pressed against me as we touched.

"As you can see, he is in my control." He spun one doll around and Jon turned around in the same direction. When the man stopped, Jon stopped. The voodoo man laughed a rich, deep laugh.

I touched Jon's face and held it in my hands. I looked deep into his vacant eyes. "Answer me."

Cher's "Dark Lady" started playing on the radio in the library, and I spun around to see the electric cord wasn't plugged into the wall.

Jon didn't blink or flinch as I held his head. He looked straight ahead, not seeing what was standing in front of him.

"What have you done to him?" I demanded. I moved around Jon and headed to the man sitting in the chair.

He held up the doll made out of blond hair. "Are you sure you want to know?" His hand squeezed harder on the doll.

I felt a pressure descend on me. I couldn't breathe. My ribs wouldn't expand to suck air into my lungs. The pressure grew as I watched his hand fist.

"What?" tried to squeak out of me.

He held his hand over the fire.

I saw hairs on his arm shrivel up and burn and my body became hotter and hotter. This wasn't happening. It was all a trick.

The doll moved closer to the flame, and a blast of smoky heat hit me in the face.

I watched as his arm tensed up. He was getting ready to throw the doll into the fire. I looked around the space and spotted a poker for the fireplace. With all the might I could muster, I dove for the poker, just as his hand released the doll. I felt free, falling in air as my fingers curled around the wooden handle. I swung blindly at the voodoo doll and connected with it.

It flew out of the fire and landed across the room from him.

My body felt like a truck hit me and threw me across a football field.

The voodoo man smiled as he raised the doll made out of black hair.

"Don't even think it." I swung the poker and slammed it into a shelf of voodoo dolls. The glass shelf shattered and dolls rained down. I swung again and again, smashing as many as I could.

The man slumped in his chair.

I wasn't sure what it was doing to him, but it felt great. Another shelf exploded in shards of glass and dolls.

He moved the arms on the doll in his hand up and thrust it in my direction.

Jon's arms rose and he lurched at me. His blind eyes searching.

I sidestepped to another wall and brought the poker down the rows of shelves.

Smash, crash, bash. Glass and voodoo dolls fell to the floor.

I moved over to the spot where my voodoo lay on the floor and quickly picked it up and slipped it into my pocket before smashing another wall of dolls.

Jon came up behind me and wrapped his arm around me, pinning my arms to my side.

I twisted and backed out of his arms. I raised the poker over my head as if to hit him.

The voodoo man sat up taller in his chair. "Do it man," his low voice growled.

I jumped around Jon's body and stood behind him. I swung the poker and hit him in the side.

Jon crumbled to the floor.

I noticed a flurry of activity in the high backed chair, as the voodoo doll man dropped his Jon doll.

I jumped over Jon and welded the poker like a samurai sword. I stooped to pick up the Jon voodoo doll and stuffed it in the pocket with my doll.

"Give them back to me," the skull faced man demanded.

Jon lay on the floor, unmoving.

I pointed to him. "How do I break the spell?"

"You can't."

Suddenly, I felt Jon's arms wrap around my body. "Are you ..."

And his hold increased.

I twisted around and faced him as his grasp held me tighter. Now I wasn't able to move. I looked into his vacant eyes and said, "I love you."

Jon squeezed harder, and his face came closer to me.

I leaned forward and kissed him. My lips sought his. I pressed my tongue into his unresponsive mouth.

Jon pushed me against the door that led out on the balcony. The French doors burst open. The floor was wet from a fine mist that started, and I found my back pressed against the railing. One of my arms was free, and I reached up. I grabbed Jon's beads, and the strands broke, sending gold, purple and green beads across the floor. I reached up again and stroking through Jon's black curls. I pulled his head to mine and kissed him.

"Finish him off," the voodoo man said. He came out onto the balcony and kicked some beads out of the way. He looked over the railing to see what I would land on.

Breaking the kiss, I looked down and saw the wrought iron fence's spears standing in a row, waiting for me as more of the beads cascaded down. Maybe I was wrong. Maybe Jon didn't love me. My tongue searched deeper and found his, as lightning shot through our bodies.

Jon held perfectly still, pressing me further over the railing, but the light was returning to his eyes.

The voodoo man moved next to us. "You can be with me, instead of him," he said into Jon's ear.

142

Jon returned the kiss I had given him, and he pulled me up and swung me around. He released me so fast that I fell to the wet floor of the balcony. Jon continued spinning and grabbed onto the voodoo man. He pushed his head over the railing and held him in place.

The voodoo man pulled his hand out of his pocket and another doll appeared. He threw it over the railing.

Jon's body rose and flew over the railing, pulling the voodoo man over with him. Jon let go of the man and grabbed onto the wet railing. He kicked and struggled to pull himself back onto the balcony, but everything was too slick.

I jumped to my feet and slipped as I reached over the railing for his arms. I pulled with all of my and felt Jon's body grow heavier.

The voodoo man grabbed around Jon's waist and pulled on him with everything he had.

Jon couldn't find a dry foothold, and he kept slipping. His arms started to slip through my wet hands.

I braced my foot against the railing and pulled, but I wasn't strong enough to get him up. His dead weight started to pull me closer to the edge.

"Help," Jon said.

I looked down to see what else I could do. Amongst the beads lay a small skeletal doll at my foot.

"I can't hang on," Jon yelled.

I stepped down hard on the doll.

The voodoo man screamed and tensed.

I kicked the doll off the balcony. Slowly, it rolled in the air, feet over head.

The voodoo man's hands released, and he flipped feet over head.

The doll landed on a spear and was pierced through the heart.

I watched as the voodoo man landed in the same position with a spear through his heart.

"Help!"

I turned away from the fence and pulled on Jon. I was losing him, I couldn't pull him up. Blindly, I let go of my right hand and pulled our voodoo dolls out of my pocket. I stretched to set them down firmly on the balcony. I pulled them closer to me and held them in place.

Jon's foot caught on an edge of the window and pushed himself up. His hand firmly caught the railing and pulled himself up. He pulled himself over the railing and landed in my arms.

"You saved me," Jon said as he kissed me.

"No," I said as I broke our kiss, "you saved us."

We walked down the stairs and out of the house. The fine rain had increased its intensity since the struggle started. The voodoo man's paint had started to run. As we walked by, I recognized the man: Richard Williamson, Jon's ex.

Jon looked down at his ex's body. "He didn't want to let me go."

I grabbed him and hugged him to my body. "I know the feeling." I kissed him and said, "Let's head back to the party."

"Maybe we should head back to our hotel."

Jon always had great ideas.

Lance Zarimba is an occupational therapist working in Minneapolis, MN. He lives in a haunted house that the man who invented Old Dutch potato chips built. It is only natural, since he grew up watching Dark Shadows in the Upper Peninsula of Michigan, and he enjoys all of the classic monster movies. He also loves mysteries and collects books. His nephew, Matthew, helped him come up with the idea for Oh No, My Best Friend is a Zombie, Oh No, Our Best Friend is a Vampire, *and* Oh No, My Brother is Frankenstein's Monster. *He has a mystery,* Vacation Therapy *and over 100 short stories. His short stories can be found in* Mayhem in the Midlands, *Pat Dennis'* Who Died in Here? 25 mystery stories of crimes and bathrooms, *Jay Hartman's* The Killer Wore Cranberry *and* Moon Shot: Murder and Mayhem on the Edge of Space, *Anne Frasier's* Deadly Treats, *and Jeani Rector's* Shadow Masters. *He can be reached at LanceZarimba@yahoo.com .*

BOURBON STREET LUCIFER
BY
ESSEL PRATT

Outside of the Cat's Meow, on the iconic Bourbon Street, the party was in full swing. Hordes of gawkers walked slowly with mouths agape at the sight of bare breasts around them. For those that had never visited the whack-a-doodle event known as Mardi Gras, it was a voyeuristic treat that garnered many unexpected surprises.

"Shouldn't we take those girls to the station? They're showing their tits to everyone. Hell, the blonde just took cash after rubbing that man's crotch for a couple minutes. Surely that can be considered prostitution," said Daniel.

"Ha ha ha, son, you have a lot to learn about Mardi Gras. If this were a normal night, then yeah, we would take them in. But if this were a normal night, they wouldn't be doing those things. Just relax and enjoy the show," said Lenny.

Lenny was a seasoned officer on the force. Despite the increased crime during Mardi Gras, he loved to patrol the streets. The laid back atmosphere allowed him to shed his tough exterior and enjoy the shift. In the process, he was willing to overlook a bit of lewd conduct in lieu of searching out bigger issues like robbery and physical violence. On the other hand, Daniel was a rookie and very by the book in his approach. His stiffness proved he was still green and his actions showed that he didn't want to look bad to his superiors.

"Tonight is going against everything I learned in the Academy, but I will say that the view is beautiful," said Daniel as a buxom brunette showed him her piercings. To return the favor, he tossed her a strand of beads that hung from a nearby tree.

"That's the spirit, now let's get moving. We don't want to loiter in one spot too long; we still need to look out for the bad stuff."

The night was abnormally hot and the humidity clung to everyone, intermixing with their sweat. Most opted to cool off with ice cold beers and chilled wine, while others stripped down to the bare minimum allowed by law. Despite the amount of drunkenness, everybody seemed to play well together for the most part. However, a scuffle near the end of the block drew the attention of a hundred, or so, onlookers.

"Damn it," yelled Lenny. "Let's go"

Everyone was shoulder to shoulder, yet the perspiring bodies allowed enough lubrication for the two officers to glide right through them on the way to the fight. As they arrived at the scene, the man on top was brutally beating the bloodied man below while yelling out obscenities and calling him 'Satan's demon' with each blow.

It took both officers to restrain the irate attacker, and a couple of minutes to place the handcuffs on him. Daniel held him face down to the ground as Lenny called for some nearby paramedics. The victim looked bad; his breathing was deep and erratic. He was no doctor, but he would be surprised if the man's spirit wasn't haunting the corner within the hour.

"Kill the goddamn demon!" yelled the attacker.

Daniel had a tough time holding him due to the slippery sweat that glistened upon his skin. To make it easier, he put on a pair of purple rubber gloves, which provided a better grip. He, and Lenny, figured the man was hopped up on acid or some other mind altering drug. Not that it mattered; the wagon had arrived in record time, and he was quickly en route to the jail to sleep off his sins.

It didn't take long to disperse the crowd from the scene and alleviate the anxiety caused by the fight. Everyone was there to have fun, so they moved on to the next bar, restaurant, and costumed lunatics. On a normal night, a beating like that would have taken hours to investigate, but during Mardi Gras, being quick was key to keep the peace.

Daniel and Lenny walked the streets for another half hour before a feathery transvestite approached them in a panic. He struggled to tell them about a fight in front of the St. Louis Cathedral. He pointed frantically muttering about an exorcism, blood, and expelling demons before running off towards the disturbance. Both officers followed in pursuit as they ran the quarter mile towards their destination.

When they arrived, the scene was similar to the one that transpired just thirty minutes prior. Once again, they tore the maniac from atop the bloodied victim as he refused to stop throwing punches. Learning from before, both officers had slipped on the rubber gloves as they ran to the scene, making it much easier to restrain the sweaty perp. This beating seemed to be much worse, and the victim died before an ambulance could arrive.

The scene was cleared of all onlookers and a barricade was placed around a thirty foot radius to ensure there was enough room to investigate. Lenny attempted to question the crazed attacker, but his speech was so slurred that the words blended together. He would be of no help until he slept off whatever chemicals he ingested.

Daniel opted to question the tranny. Although a bit overdramatic and flamboyant, he provided quite a bit of detail.

"I thought he was kind of cute, so I was watching him out of the corner of my eye. He was laughing, having fun, and drinking. You know a happy drunk. Some man with dreads and a creepy accent gave him those beads he's wearing, and within a few minutes he attacked that man wearing the red devil mask."

"So, you think the beads had something to do with it?" asked Daniel.

"I don't know, but that guy creeped me the fuck out. And he smelled, damn he smelled to high heaven of weed," responded the transvestite.

"Thank you for your help, I have your contact information; here is my card. We will contact you if we need anything else. Try to have fun tonight, and be safe," said Daniel.

Daniel returned to Lenny and shared the information. Looking at the beads around the perpetrator's neck, they realized that they were not plastic, but some sort of candy instead. Carefully, they removed them and placed them in an evidence bag. Lenny also found the devil's mask on the ground, and placed it in another bag.

"You know, there was a devil's mask near the other victim earlier. I wonder if he was wearing it?" said Lenny.

"I'm not sure, but the station just sent me a text and confirmed that the first perp was wearing the same beads. I guess we're looking for a dreadlocked man that smells of weed."

"Have you been here at all tonight? A quarter of the crowd matches that description," replied Lenny.

The two finished up their work at the scene before passing it off to the investigators. They found it hard to get back in the celebratory mood after the two incidents. As they walked their assigned blocks, their eyes gravitated towards everyone's beads and their noses sniffed the air for the pungent smell of marijuana.

For two hours they searched in vain as there were no further fights reported, nor was there any sign of the beads they searched for. They began to relax a little as the late night ushered less clothing within the stagnant swampy heat. Most of the crimes they encountered were minor; most settled upon their intrusion and a suggestion to get a hotel room.

They looked less and less for the beads, and switched their focus on those that were experiencing borderline alcohol poisoning due to the gluttonous consumption stemming from the early hours.

"She looks pretty bad. I think we need to check on her," said Daniel as he pointed towards an older blond woman kneeling just inside the shadow of nearby tree.

The two approached her as she vomited on the ground and her bare feet. Her wrinkled back, visible through her long hair, revealed that she was topless and the drooping curvature of her ass cheeks showed them that she was completely naked. She was sobbing while mumbling that she'd ruined her shoes, although they were obviously nowhere in sight. They tried to lift her by the armpit and move her to a nearby bench, but she fought their coercion.

"No, you can't make me move. I'm using the toilet," she protested.

Lenny tried to calm her, and explain that she was out in the public where everyone could see her, but she didn't care. Instead, a puddle of piss mingled with the vomit as she grunted hard. The piss was immediately followed by an eruption of diarrhea. At that point, they let her finish before forcing her to the bench. There was no sense trailing the mess along with them.

While she grunted her last expulsion, followed by a vibrato of expelling gases, Daniel removed a foil blanket from his slim backpack, which held emergency supplies for the night, and wrapped it around the older woman as she was escorted to the bench. Lenny called for paramedics, as he examined her for any signs of visible harm.

He pulled back her hair and noticed that she was wearing one of the candy necklaces, similar to the ones the attackers from earlier wore. She was not showing the same signs of aggression as the others, but was obviously not acting like a normal person. He began to wonder if she were drunk or something else.

"You two look like sound," said the woman with a smile. Her glassy eyes drifted off past them as she retreated somewhere in her mind.

"I would guess acid, by the way she is acting and talking," said Lenny.

"Lady, where did you get those beads?" asked Daniel.

She was slow to respond, but after being asked a few times she snapped into herself and pointed towards the corner of Saint Peter and Bourbon Street. It was only a block away, so they figured it was as good a place as any to begin their search anew.

The paramedics arrived and took the woman to the hospital. Despite the heat, she was not as sweaty as everyone else, possibly due to dehydration. However, she drooled quite a bit, which dribbled down her chin and neck, moistening the candy beads. Lenny had a feeling that those beads were laced with LSD or some other sort of mind altering drug. He had investigated a similar case in a local school earlier in the year, and the victims reacted similarly to this woman. With everyone so sweaty, the sugary candy was sure to melt when in contact with the skin, allowing the liquefied drug to soak into the skin.

"Man, acid treats everyone different," said Lenny to Daniel. "But, from what I have seen in the past, scary things, like those devil masks, freak the users out. They usually run away from the thing that scares them, but sometimes they fight back brutally."

"So, you're saying we need to find this guy before he passes out more beads," replied Daniel.

The two thanked the paramedics for their help and rushed to the packed corner that the woman had pointed to. The crowd was thick in this area, most likely due to the fame of the surrounding establishments. Camera flashes created a strobe effect as people took pictures of the iconic buildings and random nudity. Cheers erupted every few seconds, most likely a result of a bared tit or two.

The smell of marijuana hovered in the area, the windless air holding it in place. It wasn't the overpriced skunk type that was common during the festival; instead, it carried a flowery scent within its identifiable aroma. Since the smell was everywhere around them, it was difficult to discern where it was coming from exactly. They decided to push their way through the crowd in an attempt to locate the source.

As they neared the front of the mob, a man that matched the description emerged from the balcony above them. Two naked women, one pasty white and the other cocoa in color, both wearing featureless white masks, shook and tweaked their breasts for the crowd. Everyone went wild at the display of naughtiness, and cheers erupted.

The man with dreadlocks smiled big, showing off his gold teeth. He hid his eyes behind sunglasses. He raised his hands in the air to hype up the crowd as the cocoa-skinned woman kneeled before the other, burying her face in the shimmery white woman's overgrown muff. The crowd went insane as the scene played out in front of them.

Lenny and Daniel reached the door to the apartment above the bar, but it was locked. Lenny attempted to bust through the sturdy door, but it would not budge. Daniel suggested he

150

shoot the lock out, but he declined due to the chance of the ricochet hurting someone in the crowd. Instead, he called for backup.

While the two officers awaited help, the man above began to throw hundreds of the candy beads to the crowd, along with just as many of the devil's masks they saw earlier in the night. The crowd scrambled to get their rewards for cheering on the sexual act that played out above. Their sweaty bodies crowded together and heated up the area more than it would if they were alone on the corner, causing each to become soaked in their salty perspiration. The sugary beads dissolved upon contact with the warm sweat, sticking to the wearer's skin.

Those that grabbed the demonic masks put them on and cheered loudly in spirit of the festival, many exposing themselves, men and women, in appreciation of the show above. The rambunctious crowd trapped the two officers in the door's alcove as they danced around and chanted their hoorays.

Within minutes, the acid-laced candy beads worked their voodoo as the crowd began to freak out at those wearing the demonic masks. Their fright turned to anger as a couple of people yelled out, "kill the demons". The words instigated a massive brawl amongst those poisoned by the acid absorbed into their bodies, numbing their pains as they beat upon those wearing the masks. From their eyes, the fires of hell could be seen pulsating through the corner as the moment summoned a holy crusade against the devilish foes.

Lenny attempted to calm the crowd by firing a shot into the air above everyone, careful to avoid the wrought iron balcony above his head. The warning did little more than excite a couple of large men near him. In their tripped-out state, they grabbed the officer and pulled him into the middle of the brawl. He was defenseless as fists pounded him upon his face and feet jabbed repeatedly into his ribs. In mere minutes, he breathed his last breath.

Daniel huddled in the dark alcove, keeping low and out of the way of the mob. He shivered with fright, despite his normally cocky demeanor. He worried that he would be pulled into the mob next.

Behind him, the oak door opened without a sound, only noticeable by the air-conditioned breeze that escaped. Daniel kept his head tucked, not knowing what to expect, but a whiff of the flowery pot told him that the creator of the chaos was there.

"Hey mon, why you down so low?" he asked with an island accent. "Come inside and enjoy the party".

A large man helped to lift Daniel from the ground and manhandle him upstairs. Despite attempting to fight them off, he was quickly restrained with his own handcuffs. They used a roll of red duct tape to affix two of the devil's masks to either side of his head

The two men carried Daniel to the balcony and yelled out; "kill their leader" as they tossed him over and into the crowd. He was caught by a group of people towards the center and brutally pulled to pieces as the mob played tog-o-war with his arms and legs.

The islander and his cohorts retreated into the suite as the riot patrol appeared and began work on calming the acid-trip induced brawl. It took hours to finally restrain each of the surviving victims, and start work on sorting out those that had perished.

During the chaos, the islander slipped away via a dark alley at the rear of the building. The chaos he left behind was replayed online and on the news via the multitude of cameras in the area, not one showing his face. He was labeled the Bourbon Street Lucifer by the media. His story replayed every year on Mardi Gras, although he was never seen or heard from again, other than in local lore.

Essel Pratt has spent his life exploring his imagination and dreams. As a Husband and a Father, he doesn't always have as much time to write as he would like. However, his mind is always plotting out his next story and manipulating the plot. Someday he hopes to quit the 9-5 grind and focus on writing full time. Currently, Essel is building his catalog by contributing to various anthologies as he works on his first novel. He also contributes to www.nerdzy.com and www.infendo.com on an (almost) daily basis. Essel focuses his writings on mostly

Horror/Sci-Fi, however is known to add a bit of other genres into his writings as well. You can follow Essel at: facebook.com/esselprattwriting and Esselpratt.blogspot.com and on Twitter @EsselPratt

RED BEANS AND RICIN
BY
SARAH E. GLENN

"I still say it's blasphemy," I said. The fish, oblivious to religious matters, continued to swim in the oversized aquarium behind me.

"Nonsense," Sophia lowered the tureen into a carrier. It contained her 'famous tofu gumbo', a dish I would soon have to sample and, I hoped, manage to compliment with a straight face.

"Celebrating Mardi Gras on Ash Wednesday isn't disrespectful?"

"We're not Christians. We just like Mardi Gras and Cajun food and our group meets on Wednesdays."

I didn't recall tofu being in any Cajun dish, but I wasn't going to argue with her. She was my girlfriend and I wanted it to stay that way.

Yes, even lesbians can get whipped.

The group was called the Wednesday Madams, and they were a long-running eclectic spiritual group. This was my introduction to them, and I was nervous. They were Pagans, and I didn't know jack about Paganism. I was the detective who had kept the owner of the Ladyvisions Gallery out of prison, though, so Sophia assured me that I'd already made a good impression.

Our hostesses, Brenda and Glenda, lived in a Victorian they were restoring on Merrimon Avenue. There were several cars already parked in the driveway and behind the house. They were all highly legible, each covered with bumper stickers. Most of them were messages like "Nature is my Church" and "Harm None". The car next to the Big Blue recycling bin had a sticker with a sketched broom, underscored with the words "I Drive a Stick".

We entered through the kitchen with our offerings. A stout woman with a bun was draining a large pot into the sink. The antennae protruding through the perforated lid told me it contained crawfish. At least there would be one dish here I could eat.

Sophia wrinkled her nose, naturally. "I can't believe you made those. Didn't they scream when you threw them in?"

The stout woman chuckled and continued draining. "I wore earplugs. I started them early so their deaths wouldn't hurt your delicate sensibilities."

"That was very nice of you... for me, at least. I'm not so sure about them."

The stout woman set the pot down and turned around to face me. "Is this your new girlfriend?"

"Yes, this is Lana. Lana, meet Brenda."

"Pleased to meet you," I said, grasping her outstretched hand. It was hot and moist from the steam, but felt strong.

"And you. Set your dishes down on the counter there, ladies. I presume that's your gumbo, Sophia. Did you bring the filé?"

"Right here." She lifted the bottle of dusky powder with a slender hand.

"Put it on the tray with the hot sauces. What's the other one? Does it need to be warmed up?"

"Red beans and rice," I said. "Vegan. I didn't know if anyone in the group ate meat."

"That depends on the phase of the moon. Good choice, though. My sister loves red beans and rice."

The dining room, fully restored, was draped with shiny metallic banners. Brandy snifters filled with colorful beads flanked the clock on the mantle. The purple paper tablecloth on the table was sprinkled with Mardi Gras confetti that looked like the type my cousin Allie picked up at the dollar store for her own party.

A cough interrupted my inspection. Brenda entered from the nearby parlor, which was on the other end of the dining room. Her hair was loose, falling to her shoulders in brown and gray waves. She'd changed from the black pantsuit and apron she'd worn in the kitchen to a purple muumuu. "Happy Fat Wednesday!" she announced. "Is this your new girlfriend, Sophia?"

Sophia laughed when she saw the confused look on my face. "This is Glenda, Brenda's sister. Twins."

"Brenda and Glenda," I repeated.

"I'm the good witch," Glenda said with a smile. And another cough.

More women entered from the kitchen, including one I recognized. I was taken aback. So was Sophia. Her already fair complexion paled further.

"Celeste," she said after a moment.

"Sophia," Celeste replied, without inflection. "I hope you've been well."

Who had invited Sophia's ex to the same gathering as me? I was the detective Sophia had hired to confirm Celeste Moonbow's infidelity, and now I was Sophia's girlfriend as well. Maybe they wanted to have a show with dinner.

Celeste swept past me without comment, midnight brown hair and flowing sleeves trailing behind her. "Glenda, dear, what do you have planned for us this evening?"

Glenda kissed the ex's cheek, lowering my opinion of her. "Nothing too fancy, since we have newbies."

"Ah, yes," Celeste said, glancing in my direction. "Outer court."

Obviously some sort of in-joke.

The other women introduced themselves, breaking up the uncomfortable moment.

"I'm so very pleased to meet you," a blonde woman with a tat sleeve of roses told me. "You believed Ananda when no one else did. And saved the Ladyvisions Gallery, too."

"Morgana does some great metalwork," Sophia said. "You should see her version of Artemis in iron."

I shook her hand; her grip was stronger than mine. "I'm pleased to meet you, too. Do you also exhibit at Ananda's gallery?"

"Not yet. But she's promised me a show when I have a few more large pieces for display." She turned back to Sophia. "How is the painting going?"

"I'm working on a more personal project right now. A portrait of Lana on the spiritual plane."

Morgana glanced back at me. "What do you think of it?"

"It shows a side of me I never knew." Especially the part that was a bear. "I'm waiting to see what it looks like when she's done."

"You are so lucky."

"Come into the kitchen, ladies, and get your dishes. It's time for the feast to begin."

I studied the women as they brought their bowls and pots into the dining room and sorted out the proper spoons, forks, and ladles to put beside each. The group was a mix of older women – probably the original members – and some younger ones.

Glenda and Brenda had both disappeared upstairs. When they returned, Brenda was dressed in fringes and beads. She'd added feathers to her bun, and a beautiful silver and turquoise necklace completed the outfit.

"Another trip to Cherokee?" an older woman with freckles asked. "Haven't seen that necklace before."

Brenda started to respond, but was interrupted by the descent of her twin, also adorned with feathers and a more modest agate bola.

"Good news—well, sort of," she said. "I checked my steroid and I hadn't taken my dose today. I thought I had, but numbers don't lie."

"Numbers?" I whispered to Sophia.

"She has one of those daily inhaler disks for asthma. It has a number that shows which dose you're on so you know when you're out."

That explained the coughing.

We sat around the table. Brenda brought in two pitchers of tea – one sweetened, the other unsweetened – and her sister brought in a tray of bread and butter. After setting the bread on the table, Glenda disappeared into the kitchen again and reappeared with the tray of hot sauces. One bottle was dark and had a skull on it. Glenda stopped by her seat and dropped that bottle off there.

When we began eating, I discovered that my concept of 'spicy' was different from most of the Madams. I'd modified a vegan recipe I'd found online to make my red beans and rice. Since it didn't have sausage, I'd had to improvise to get the zing.

"These are the hottest beans I've ever eaten," Brenda said, fanning her mouth. "Did you put habaneros in them or something?"

"No. I'm sorry; I didn't realize they were too hot for the group. I grew up in a family where they practically put Texas Pete in the baby bottle."

"I think they're delicious," Sophia said.

Celeste snorted, flaring the broad nostrils. "You have to say that; she's your girlfriend."

Sophia's delicate, arched brows wrinkled. "They are good. I had far spicier when I lived in Taos."

"Well, you must have burned your taste buds away," Morgana said. "They're killing me."

"Try adding more rice," I suggested.

"Don't listen to them, Lana," Glenda said, adding a squirt of red to her dish from the dark bottle. "I love it."

"I can't believe you're adding more heat." Morgana scraped the beans to the side of her plate and took a crawfish.

"I need to clear my sinuses," Glenda said. "All I've done today is cough."

"Here, have some of my gumbo," Sophia lifted the china tureen. "Maybe it'll soothe your throat."

Glenda took a bowlful and reached for the filé powder. "I've heard sassafras has tonic properties. Couldn't hurt."

I murmured my hope that she would feel better and decided to take the plunge myself. "Let me have some gumbo, too. I need to see why it's famous."

My girlfriend laughed and ladled out a generous portion. "Don't forget the filé."

It wasn't bad. It could have used some shrimp and some Andouille sausage, but it wasn't bad. Really. The tofu was smoked, but it was still… tofu. I wondered what a tofu smoker would look like. An ice cube tray with a lid?

The jambalaya was disappearing quickly, which I took as a sign of tastiness. My guess was correct. "Who made this? It's great."

"You have another fan," Morgana said to the freckled woman opposite me. "I hear you did very well in the Cajun Cook-off this year, Olivia."

"If you served this, I'm not surprised."

"Thanks."

I eyed the crawfish. Should I, or shouldn't I?

Sophia nudged me. "Oh, go ahead," she said. "Just wash up well before we leave. My fish will smell you and get nervous."

Once the King Cake had been shared and one Tsula Firemountain had discovered the Baby in her piece, we moved to the parlor. Everyone took out drums and rattles while Glenda lit some incense. I didn't think that was a good idea, but it was her house and her lungs.

"Here, Lana," Sophia handed me a gourd from her bag. Webbing studded with cowrie shells and small bells covered it, making small tinkling sounds as I turned it over. She chose a wooden frog and drumstick for herself.

Next to us, the Madams' single African-American member unveiled a drum with a furry skin. It drew looks from the other members.

"New drum, Jada? You didn't shave the head?" Tsula asked.

"I planned to," Jada said, "but I really like the way the fur feels. Almost like having a pet. It makes a nice muted sound, too."

Glenda brought a bag from a corner and reached inside. She pulled out necklaces. "To keep us in the proper mood. Brenda and I have been working on these for the last week. Here's yours, Morgana, and yours, Celeste..."

"I love the carved wood beads. Are these beans strung between them?" Morgana asked. "Yes, those are coral beans," Glenda said. "Here, Tsula. This is yours."

Tsula placed her gift, a strand of round black beans alternated with oval speckled beans, around her neck.

Sophia's was a strand of white beans and blue glass beads. It looked lovely on her, of course. I was handed a necklace with big round... somethings.

"Thank you. What are these?"

"Those are nickernuts, with tamarind seeds in between."

The name produced a laugh, but a good-natured one. I draped it around my neck.

Brenda produced the final strand. "And for Jada, of course, we have coffee beans."

Jada grinned. "I am a caffeine fiend."

Once everyone had donned their gifts, Glenda moved to the center of the room. "Everyone calm down," she said. "Time to set aside chatter and focus. Focus on your breath." She coughed, and got a few sympathy coughs in response. "Breathe in... breathe out. Focus."

Some of the women closed their eyes. Glenda looked up, but I didn't think she was examining the old chandelier.

"We gather here again, in celebration," she intoned. "The winter is ending and spring will soon be upon us. We celebrate the joys of the holidays, now past, and the blessings to come. Who will share some of their blessings with us?"

"I've been promoted," Celeste announced. "I'm taking over the Henderson branch, now that Brenda is retiring."

Henderson branch? Wait—Stevenson. Stevenson Laundromats. No wonder the twins could afford to renovate

Victorian houses. I'd used the Henderson Road branch myself when I'd lived out that way. I dimly remembered Brenda now—a little thinner, less gray in the hair. A fondness for turquoise even then. Guess I wasn't going back there any time soon.

Other people shared their good news. Olivia was going to be a grandmother in June, which prompted speculations about whether the baby would be a Gemini or a 'Moon Child'. Another woman had just become an aunt.

"I have Lana," Sophia gave as her blessing, which made me flush and produced another flare from Celeste's nostrils.

"Let's celebrate our blessings, then, and make a joyful noise," Glenda concluded. "Let the drumming commence, and let us share our love and blessings with others."

Morgana set the pace with a large drum shaped like a goblet. The others joined in. Jada was right about her new 'pet' – it set up a nice counterpoint to the ringing echo of the big drum. My gourd made a nice sound, but I was glad other people had rainsticks and rattles to drown me out. I hadn't played with stuff like this since kindergarten.

I was doing my best to keep time when Glenda abruptly set down her drum and dashed from the room. The drumming continued, but slowed when Sophia left the circle as well. She knocked on the bathroom door, then raced up the stairs.

There was a sudden rumble in my own guts. Uh-oh.

"Your beans did not make everyone sick," Sophia said during the drive home. "Celeste was just saying that to get your goat."

The party had abruptly ended with lines at both bathrooms and plenty of bad sentiment. "Everyone else thought it was the beans, too."

"There were lots of other spicy foods," she replied. "Unless you added something really weird to your beans, they weren't the cause."

"It's a big coincidence."

"What spices do you use? Is it a family recipe?"

"No, I modified a vegan recipe from the Internet. I added a little more spice than they recommended and left out the kale."

162

"Why would you leave out the kale?"

She was asking the question sincerely. I'd left it out because the idea of adding kale to red beans and rice was ridiculous. Couldn't say that, though, so... "The kale I saw at the co-op didn't look fresh enough."

"Oh." Suddenly, Sophia pulled the car over to the shoulder and jumped out.

"What's up?" I asked, as she ran for the bushes.

Damn. I'd really poisoned her.

I stayed over at Sophia's place in Biltmore Forest. I was better by the next morning, but Sophia continued to have problems. I didn't want to leave her alone, so I called Allie and told her to just take messages for the time being. I'd brought Sophia some bottled water when Captain Vickers arrived. Not good. He was smiling, which was worse.

"Haven't seen you in a while Fisher... how're you doing these days?"

"Well enough," I said uncomfortably.

"Hear you're doing some detective work out of some strip mall."

"Nothing fancy, sir. I don't think you'll be out of business any time soon."

He laughed that braying laugh I hated. "No, we have too much going on. For example, someone who died from your beans."

I felt sick again. "From my beans?"

Vickers made a great show of pulling out a report pad. "I understand you and some other no-men types were having a party for Ash Wednesday when people started getting sick."

Sophia had turned paler. "Died?"

"Yes, a Miss Glenda Stevenson passed away last night at Mission. Real bad death."

Sophia's aquamarine eyes turned glassy. "Glenda. Oh, Goddess." She felt around with her delicate hand for the tissues on the table, and I handed the box to her. She grabbed one and pressed it to her eyes.

163

"Detective Ross has been handling most of the interviews, but I thought I'd come do this one myself, seeing's how it involves one of our own. Or at least a used-to-be one of our own." His gaze shifted back to me.

"I wouldn't use the term 'involves'," I said. "It was my first time meeting the group."

"And it could be the last, based on what they've been telling us."

My back stiffened. "What did they say?"

"A bunch of them think it was the red beans and rice you brought. It was real spicy. One—" he checked his notes, "One Lester Moonbeam said the victim—one of the victims—got sick a short time after eating it. Strange, it says Lester's a girl here. Maybe she didn't start life that way."

He leered at me, but I didn't rise to the bait. "People don't die from spicy food." Did they?

"Captain, that's just nonsense," Sophia said. "Glenda and I would both have died many years ago."

"She's dead now. But you're right—the state lab is examining the contents of Miss Stevenson's party trash. Could be that the taste was covering up something else. If you like hot food as much as the victim did, Miss Farris, maybe you were the intended victim. I'd watch the people close to you, especially the ones who cook."

And with that little added fillip, he left.

Vickers hadn't liked me before he learned my sexual orientation, and his verbal abuse of me had gotten just shy of harassment on the job before I left the department. That was back in the days when most people in North Carolina still turned a blind eye when the victim was gay or lesbian. Since then, he'd moved up in the ranks. His assumptions, combined with Celeste's stirring the pot, were going to cause serious trouble.

Sophia kept reassuring me that my food hadn't been the cause of anyone's illness, but I wondered.

And worried. Sophia was still sick. She kept pushing fluids, which was good, but I couldn't forget poor Glenda.

She'd been eating leftover gumbo to supplement the water and herbal tea. After another episode in the bathroom, she came out and picked up her bottle of filé powder. She examined and then opened it.

"Lana? Smell this."

I sniffed. "Sorry, this isn't my forte. Smells like leaves."

"It should, but it doesn't smell much like sassafras. I thought it was just a weak batch, but now I'm thinking it's not filé powder at all. I've gotten sick every time I've eaten my gumbo today."

Since she wanted to stay close to the toilet, I was the one deputized to take the suspicious bottle to Jim Bearcat for closer examination. Jim lived the next town over, but he spent a good deal of time in Asheville these days visiting Ananda, the owner of the Ladyvisions gallery. A quick phone call later, I was headed for Asheville's downtown. Downtown is distinguished by its Art Deco architecture and a number of shops catering to the city's more eclectic citizens. The gallery, located near Malaprop's bookstore, specialized in New Age and Native American-inspired art.

Ananda, better known to me as Amanda Calder, greeted me when I came in. "I just heard about Glenda. I'm so very sorry."

"I am, too." I really, really hoped she wouldn't ask me about the beans. "Where's Jim?"

"He's been finishing his lunch in the back." She ushered me into the office, where Jim Bearcat was eating quinoa out of a Tupperware container.

"Hey, how you been, Lana? Isn't that Sophia Farris's hat?" He pointed to the lavender fedora I was wearing.

"She insisted I wear it. She thinks it's lucky."

"It was lucky for Ananda. Doesn't sound like it was lucky for Glenda. I heard everyone got sick last night."

The grapevine in Asheville's New Age community wasn't telepathic, but pretty damned fast. "They complained that my beans were too hot, but I've eaten worse."

165

"It wouldn't be the spice, unless you used something Glenda was allergic to."

Another lovely thing to worry about. "Sophia sent me over to do an herbal consult."

"Herbalism's my specialty. Show me the bogus sassafras."

I handed him the bottle, and he sniffed it. "It's got some sassafras, I can smell it. Although I guess that could be because the bottle held sassafras at one time. Sort of weak. Something else there, though, something familiar." He lifted a pinch of the brown powder and sniffed it, then put it in his mouth.

"Are you sure that's wise?" I asked, but he was already spitting it out into Amanda's wastebasket.

"It still has a little sassafras in it, but someone's played a trick on you—or at least Sophia. This is senna."

Senna was an herb used in many laxative medicines, so the sudden onslaught after the feast made sense. Jim didn't think that anyone would have died from the normal amount sprinkled on gumbo, but Glenda had already been sick. Maybe she'd been sicker than she'd thought, and the addition of a laxative was too much for her body to handle.

Sophia was furious when she discovered what had been in the bottle. It was amazing how cute she made flushed cheeks and a stern chin look. "It has to have been Celeste."

"I'm sure it was, but we can't prove it. We can't fingerprint it."

"The police can," she said. "We should report this tampering."

"Sophia," I protested, "everyone at dinner last night would have used this on their gumbo. Everyone's fingerprints will be on it."

"Not Celeste's. She turned her nose up when I offered it to her. I thought she was just being snitty, but now I know that she knew what was going to happen."

"Uh huh. The police will not be impressed."

She'd already picked up the phone. "I need to speak to Captain Vickers. I've discovered that someone tampered with the food last night."

Vickers was over in a trice. I was impressed. He deflated when Sophia held up the filé bottle and informed him that it held a laxative.

"You reported it as a food tampering. That's just a gag."

"This 'gag' could have killed someone. Maybe it did. Glenda was sick and she ate some of it to feel better. Instead, it killed her."

"That's not what she died from," he said, and then snapped his mouth shut.

"She had the same symptoms everyone else had. Dehydration is a serious matter."

I was more impressed by his sudden silence than any dehydration. "Do they know what *did* kill her... Sir?"

"You'll find out when the coroner makes his public statement, Fisher. That's what you are now, public. Calling me over here with a bullshit story about gumbo."

The aquamarine eyes flashed. "She did not call you, Captain, I called you," Sophia said. "As a courtesy. I could have called the Biltmore Forest Police and let them handle this investigation, since it was my food that was tainted."

The Biltmore Forest Police saw to the needs of the residents of Biltmore Forest, a town set entirely within Asheville. It was small, but it contained some of the wealthiest residents of North Carolina.

Vickers knew that too, and ratcheted his attitude down. "I'm sorry, ma'am. You were right to call me. Miss Stevenson was an Asheville resident and I am responsible for the investigation into her death. It's just that a laxative--"

We were interrupted by a heavy thump on the front door. Sophia went to open it and returned with a man in a dark suit.

Vickers scowled at the man. The man scowled back, then turned to me.

"Roy Waddle, ma'am. I'm from the Charlotte FBI office."

During my brief time with the Asheville Police, I'd never been in a position to meet anyone from Charlotte. This fellow looked young enough to still be in high school. Or was it just my age?

"Miss—is it Miss? Farris reported a food tampering. I'd like to learn more."

Something was definitely wrong in the state of North Carolina. Vickers was treating the incident exactly the way I expected him to, but he'd seemed unusually excited when he'd arrived. Now someone from Charlotte was here and Vickers really had his nose out of joint."

"What did kill Glenda?" I asked again, but I was ignored. What else was new?

Waddle took Sophia's statement and Vickers followed suit. There was a brief disagreement as to which representative of The Law was going to take custody of the senna, but Waddle won when he alluded to the Department already having taken possession of the other party leftovers. Vickers looked like an angry frog when he said it.

This was much, much more serious than I'd thought. I thought it best to let Vickers and Waddle handle matters—they had the resources and apparently didn't suspect us any more—but Sophia disagreed, at least about the filé powder.

"We need to go grill some suspects," she proclaimed, taking the fedora from the couch and adjusting it to the right angle on her head.

"Prepare to be bored first," I replied. "We need to make a list of the people who attended and what they ate. It probably was Celeste, but we can't rule anyone else out."

"I'm already there," she said, indicating her tablet. "They're on a spreadsheet. I worked on it while you were gone."

Holy shit. I looked it over. One shrimp étouffée, one seitan étouffée (I didn't want to think about that one too hard), two jambalayas, two gumbos (one vegan, the other not), two dishes of red beans and rice (one vegan, the other not), one dish of pecan pralines, one King Cake, and one plate of beignets.

Celeste claimed she'd made the latter, but they looked an awful lot like the ones from that place on College Street.

"This is very good," I said. "I see that Brenda didn't eat the gumbo either. That makes her a possible suspect."

"She doesn't like tofu or seitan."

"But Celeste would be the first to point it out if we accused her without doing a full investigation," I said. She looked so damned cute in that hat. "She was also in the kitchen when people were putting their dishes there. If she's not a suspect, she's at least a witness."

"Good idea," she said, kissing my cheek. "We'll get the goods on Celeste and then grill her. Let's go."

"Her sister just died," I said. "I don't think she'll be up to visitors any time soon."

"Then we'll go to offer our condolences," she said, "but remember, the senna might be what killed her in the first place. She'd want to know."

I wasn't so sure, but I was overruled. Again.

The Victorian was in understandable disarray when Brenda let us in. Her face was red, and so were her eyes. She scooped books and papers off the couch so we could sit.

Sophia was all sympathy. "I'm so very, very sorry, Brenda. I didn't realize she was so sick."

"It's been horrible." Brenda sat in one of the overstuffed armchairs. "First she was sick, then everyone was sick. I thought it was just one of those bugs and we'd all caught it from each other."

"That seems logical," Sophia said, touching her arm lightly. "But it must have been something else, mustn't it?"

Brenda jerked her arm away. "Not you, too!"

"Me, too?"

"The police were here this morning. They took all the trash from the party. They took all of Glenda's medicines. They wouldn't tell me why."

"I'm not sure that this has anything to do with the police," Sophia said, "but I discovered why everyone got sick at the party."

Brenda paled. "What? There was something wrong?"

"Yes. I discovered that someone messed with my filé powder. Jim Bearcat checked it and told us that it had been switched with senna."

She sucked in air heavily, and I reached out to steady her. I looked to Sophia, and saw that she was staring at the two of us with a puzzled expression.

"Senna?" Brenda sputtered after a moment. Then, she laughed. "Senna? But why? Oh, Goddess." The tears were back.

"I think someone played what they thought was a joke," I said.

Sophia added, "I've reported it to the police."

"Of course you have." Brenda grabbed a tissue and pressed it to her mouth. "What did they say?"

"The fellow from the FBI took the bottle. You know it doesn't normally… it doesn't kill people. But, I thought, if she were already sick and got dehydrated…"

"Yes. Thank you for telling me. I've been blaming myself, you know. I thought—maybe if I'd taken it more seriously, if I hadn't thought it was just a bug…"

"Glenda was always so strong. You thought she would shake it off," Sophia said. "I think we need to find the culprit, though. You were in the kitchen when people dropped off their food. Did anyone act strangely? Take an extra interest in the tray where the filé was?"

Brenda sat up straight and pressed her hands together. "I'm not sure. More than one person checked out the hot sauces. That bottle with the skull always gets a look or two. Olivia brought some of her fake salt and added it to the tray."

"Blood pressure?"

"I think so. Nothing else, but… wait. Celeste picked up the filé powder."

Sophia leaned forward in earnest, and I was afraid she would appear too eager. "You saw her pick it up?"

"No, I turned around to get some paper towels and she was holding it. She said something like, 'I see the witch brought her gumbo again'." Brenda half-smiled. "Except she used a word that rhymed with witch. What an idiot I was not to guess."

The pale cheeks were flushing again. "Did anyone else show an interest in the filé?"

"No, just her."

Celeste had recently moved into a tony neighborhood out Long Shoals Road, probably in anticipation of a greater income. Sophia muttered to herself during our drive. I figured she was going to rip into her ex-girlfriend as soon as the condo door opened, but Celeste's face stopped her. Hell, even I felt sorry for her, and I was the one whose beans had been maligned.

She slumped in the doorway and looked at our feet. Her face was puffy and her eyes had been rubbed at least one too many times. The outfit with the flowing sleeves had been replaced with a yellow sweat suit.

"If you came because of what I said to the cop, I'm sorry. I just didn't know what else to say."

"You could have told him about the senna," Sophia said. "Instead, you blamed Lana."

"I couldn't," Celeste said, and stifled a sob. "I was so terrified. You know I didn't mean to hurt anyone."

"Yes, you did," Sophia said, "but it was me you wanted to hurt."

"I didn't mean to kill her!" Celeste blurted, and began crying for real. She retreated into her condo and we followed. Posters covered the walls. One of Machu Picchu overlooked the futon she collapsed onto.

Sophia relented. "You didn't kill her."

"Yes, I did. I thought it would just be a joke, but I killed someone."

"No, you didn't," I said.

Celeste shoved her hair behind one of her ears and fixed her dark eyes on me. "I would think you would be the first to say I did."

The urge was certainly there, but I didn't believe it. "It's a temptation, but other people ate a lot more and they're still around."

"And mad," Sophia added.

"I'm—I'm very sorry," Celeste said. "It was stupid. I was just so mad about what happened, even though it was my own fault."

My girlfriend patted her ex's arm. "I forgive you; I still have a lot of anger, even though I'm with Lana. You forgive her too, don't you, Lana?"

Sophia was looking at me expectantly. Shit. "Yes, I forgive you too."

This brought more tears. "Thank you."

"What happened, happened. We need to move on with our lives."

"I'm going to lose my job," Celeste moaned.

"I'm sure Brenda isn't going to fire you," Sophia said. "With Glenda gone, she'll have to postpone her retirement, but she's going to need you even more for the Hendersonville Road store."

"It'll go under in six months with her in charge. I signed a two-year lease on this place. Oh, Goddess."

"Justin is still doing the accounting, isn't he? He can offer her financial advice if she needs it."

"The first thing she'll do is get rid of Justin."

"Why?"

She told us.

When we got back to Sophia's place, I phoned Allie from my cell. I had her run a credit check on the Stevenson twins while I accessed the Secretary of State's website on Sophia's tablet. I wanted to verify some things before I contacted one Captain Vickers.

I assigned Sophia to contact Glenda's accountant, one Justin Harwood. If anyone could weasel information of him, it was her.

After gathering several pertinent facts, I put a call in to the Department. Sophia made miso soup while we waited; she'd been put off her gumbo for the time being.

Vickers sounded unhappy when he called. What else was new?

"Hope you're not planning to waste my time again, Fisher. I have real work to do."

"I'm calling to make a trade with you. A motive for a cause of death."

"Like I said before, you're a member of the public now. You don't get special treatment."

"Oh, shucks," I said. "I guess this means I'll be calling that nice FBI agent with my information. I wanted to give my old department a leg up on the competition, but if you're going to be hostile..."

"I'm not hostile."

"You've always been hostile, bless your heart. But I wasn't going to hold it against you."

I heard muttering on the other end of the line. "I take it you don't think your friend was right about the cause of death."

"No. Because the FBI doesn't get involved with laxative poisonings."

Sophia watched as I dealt with his hemming and hawing. "No, you're going to tell me first. Because I know you'll welch, that's why. Okay, Sophia, give me Agent Waddle's card. Oh, really? Yes that would get their attention."

I looked over at my girlfriend, who was looking in her purse. "You won't have to get the card after all, dear. It was ricin. In her lungs. The doctors at the hospital thought her death was unusual and alerted the authorities."

My girlfriend dropped the bag. "Wow."

"Thank you so much, Captain. All right, here we go: The Stevenson sisters inherited the laundry business from their father, but the deceased bought her sister out last year. Brenda Stevenson is fond of visiting Cherokee, especially the casinos. She didn't stop there, though. She got involved in private games in places where there were no checks or balances."

"Do you have proof of this?"

"The part about the private games is testimony from Celeste Moonbow, whose legal name is Kaylee Lobdel." I'd forgiven Celeste, but that didn't mean I would forget. "Ross should have her other contact information. Brenda declared bankruptcy last year, which is verifiable. Her bank contested the

173

discharge of several cash advances on her credit cards because they were so recent to the bankruptcy. She was able to pay those debts off with the money she got for selling her half of the business."

"You said you had a real motive for something that happened this week, not last year. Sounds like she'd solved her problem."

"Sophia has spoken to Justin Harwood, the accountant of the business. He would only tell her so much, but Brenda's retirement wasn't voluntary. Seems it was a matter of retiring or being fired. He strongly suggested that a subpoena of the business accounts would show that the Hendersonville Road facility had come up short on income from the last quarter."

"Dammit, Fisher, I need more than that."

While we were talking, Sophia had taken possession of the tablet. She was holding the screen up to me, showing me a picture of beans. Speckled brown beans.

"Castor beans. The source of ricin," she said.

"What if I could put some physical evidence in your hands? For example, proof that the sister had recent access to the poison?"

Vickers gave me a hmm. "Go on."

I told him about Tsula's gift from the twins. "I think Brenda used some of the beans to make the poison. I also think I know the delivery system. Glenda used an inhaled steroid for her asthma. She told us she thought she had missed her dose that day, but I think she'd had one. Inhaled steroid from a plastic disc. It has numbers to show the dose you're on." I smiled at Sophia. "Either you or the FBI has the legit disc. I think there's a second disc, the one that contained the poison. She made a switch the day of the party so there'd be witnesses to Glenda's becoming ill."

I could hear the click of a keyboard through my cell. "I can tell you that we've searched their place pretty thoroughly," Vickers said. "We only found one disc like you're describing, and Waddle has it."

"Brenda let them have that one. It's probably the good disc." My mind clicked through memories of the party. Had she

174

gotten rid of the evidence before we arrived? Wait. "Has anyone checked the recycle bin?"

"What?"

"It's plastic, it's outside of the house. She could have carried it out with the recyclables without making a special trip."

My guess was correct. Vickers found the disc and took credit for cracking the case. That was fine; he knew who had made him look good. Maybe he'd be nicer to me in the future.

We learned the rest by reading the details of her confession in the Asheville Citizen-Times. Brenda had solved her immediate problem by selling her half of the business, but she had continued to gamble, and to lose money. She'd paid off some of the debt by embezzling from the store she managed, leading to her forced retirement, but it wasn't enough. She owed money to organized crime, and its agents had contacted Glenda, wanting the rest of the cash her sister owed. Glenda threatened to report them to the police, and the agents gave Brenda a choice: solve the problem with Glenda, or they'd solve the problem with both of them their way. Brenda wanted to live.

"You know," Sophia said, "if Celeste hadn't messed with my filé powder, we wouldn't have investigated what happened, and the case wouldn't have been solved."

"I'm sure they would have solved it eventually," I said. "They're not idiots, you know."

"I'm not so sure about Captain Vickers," she replied. "I suppose we should be grateful to Celeste for speeding things up."

She saw my face then. "Or, maybe not."

Sarah E. Glenn, a product of the suburbs, has a B.S. in Journalism, which is redundant if you think about it. She loves writing mystery and horror stories, often with a sidecar of funny. Several have appeared in mystery and paranormal anthologies, including G.W. Thomas' Ghostbreakers *series,* Futures Mysterious Anthology Magazine, *and* Fish Tales: The Guppy Anthology. *She belongs to Sisters in Crime, SinC Guppies, the Short Mystery Fiction Society, and the Historical Novel Society.*

Sarah was born in Asheville, North Carolina, which is known for the Biltmore House, its Art Deco downtown, and its eclectic community.

www.ingramcontent.com/pod-product-compliance
Lightning Source LLC
Chambersburg PA
CBHW072142170626
46813CB00004BA/1645